P9-DMG-607

Invisible

Also by Pete Hautman

Godless

Sweetblood

Hole in the Sky

No Limit

Mr. Was

Invisible

PETE HAUTMAN

HENRY COUNTY LIBRARY SYSTEM
COCHRAN PUBLIC LIBRARY
4802 N. HENRY BLVD.
STOCKBRIDGE, GA 30281

SIMON & SCHUSTER BOOKS FOR YOUNG READERS
New York   London   Toronto   Sydney

HENRY COUNTY LIBRARY SYSTEM
HAMPTON, LOCUST GROVE, McDONOUGH, STOCKBRIDGE

SIMON & SCHUSTER BOOKS FOR YOUNG READERS
An imprint of Simon & Schuster Children's Publishing Division
1230 Avenue of the Americas, New York, New York 10020

This book is a work of fiction. Any references to historical events,
real people, or real locales are used fictitiously. Other names,
characters, places, and incidents are products of the author's
imagination, and any resemblance to actual events or locales
or persons, living or dead, is entirely coincidental.

Copyright © 2005 by Pete Hautman
All rights reserved, including the right of reproduction in
whole or in part in any form.

SIMON & SCHUSTER BOOKS FOR YOUNG READERS
is a trademark of Simon & Schuster, Inc.
Book design by Ann Zeak.
The text for this book is set in Bembo.
Interior illustrations by Pete Hautman
Manufactured in the United States of America
2 4 6 8 10 9 7 5 3 1
Library of Congress Cataloging-in-Publication Data
Hautman, Pete, 1952–
Invisible / Pete Hautman.— 1st ed.
p. cm.
Summary: Doug and Andy are unlikely best friends—one a loner
obsessed by his model trains, the other a popular student involved
in football and theater—who grew up together and share a bond
that nothing can sever.
ISBN 0-689-86800-6 (hardcover)
[1. Best friends—Fiction. 2. Friendship—Fiction. 3. Railroads—
Models—Fiction. 4. Models and modelmaking—Fiction.
5. Schools—Fiction. 6. Mental illness—Fiction.] I. Title.
PZ7.H2887In 2005
[Fic]—dc22   2004002484

Contents

Invisible

1

MY BEST FRIEND

There is something about trains. The sound they make. The way they go by, one car after another after another after another. Every car different but somehow the same. And the tracks go on forever, connecting places, connecting people. Wherever you are, you could go to the nearest railroad track right now, and if you followed it long enough, you would find me.

There is another thing to know about trains. They are large and dangerous. They would crush you if they could, but they are confined by those two narrow strips of steel. Trains are like fire. You don't want to get in their way.

My grandfather left me his HO scale model railroad when he passed on. One locomotive, seven cars, and sixteen feet of track. That's another reason I like trains—they connect me to him, wherever he is. You could say that my railroad, the Madham Line, is almost the most important thing in my life. Next to Andy Morrow, my best friend.

A guy like Andy might have more than one best friend. He is so popular that there are at least five kids at school who would probably claim him. But if you asked Andy who was *his* best friend, *he* would say, "Dougie Hanson, of course." And that would be me.

I'm a quiet kid, pretty much invisible—except if you happen to notice me standing next to Andy. We grew up together, Andy and me. Next door, actually. We met at the age of one year and three months. Our birthdays are only seventeen days apart. We are like Velcro, like two poles of a magnet, like peanut butter and jelly, like superglue. We are best friends by every definition. Best friends. Best. Friends.

It doesn't matter to Andy Morrow that I have crooked teeth and poor coordination and wear stupid clothes. It wouldn't matter if I had a nose like a pig and smelled of Limburger cheese. Andy would *still* say, "Dougie is my best friend."

True, Andy might spend more time with other kids who *claim* to be his best friend. He might hang with the other football players, and his friends on the student council, and his golfing friends, and his theater friends, but he always comes home at night and opens his bedroom window and calls out across the low picket fence, "Hey, Dougie!"

And if my window is open, and if I'm awake, we talk.

It does not matter that we don't spend as much time together as we used to. I tell Andy all about the new tank car I bought for the Madham Line. I might talk about my mother's latest crossword puzzle, or a book I read about black holes, or a math test I took in school, and Andy would listen. That is what best friends do.

And if Andy wants to talk about the school play he is starring in, or his latest football game, or a girl he met . . . I'll listen to him, too.

It does not matter to Andy that we live in completely different realities. I'm Andy's best friend. It does not matter to Andy that we hardly ever actually *do* anything together.

Why should it? We are best friends, me and Andy. Best. Friends.

2

STELLA

My full and proper name is Douglas MacArthur Hanson. I am named after Douglas MacArthur, the famous general, who was a second cousin of my father's great-aunt. Everyone on my father's side is named after some famous person we are supposedly related to. My father's name is Henry Clay Hanson. Henry Clay was a politician who died before the Civil War. He was my grandfather's cousin's great-uncle. Or something like that. It goes on and on. Since my grandfather's name was George Washington Hanson, I guess I'm related to the father of our country too. Anyway, I'm glad I got named after a general instead of a politician. I think it makes me sound more respectable.

Usually when I meet someone for the first time, I tell them my full and proper name. Then I say, "But you can call me General." Some people find that amusing. Andy always laughs. Sometimes he calls me General, just to tease me. I don't mind. I kind of like it. I am very easy to get along with.

My mother would not agree with that. She finds me difficult. In fact, she thinks that I am troubled and disturbed. I find it troubling that she finds me disturbing, so she must be right.

Right?

"Hey, Dougie!"

I look at my alarm clock: 1:17.

"Dougie, you up?"

I roll out of bed and crawl to the window.

"I'm up now," I say, resting my chin on the windowsill.

"How's it going?" Andy is sitting in his window, his long legs dangling over the spirea bushes.

"I was dreaming."

"What were you dreaming?"

"I don't remember. Hey, was tonight your play?"

"Yeah! It went great. I didn't miss a line. But—you're gonna like this—Melissa's skirt came off."

"Melissa Haverman?"

"Yeah! See, I'm Stanley Kowalski, and Melissa is playing Stella, my wife? And in this one scene she's really mad and she spins around fast and the bottom of her skirt gets caught on a nail sticking out of this table leg and it comes right off." He laughs. "She was wearing blue panties."

I have a very vivid imagination. I can see it in my head just like a movie.

Andy says, "But she was really cool. She grabbed the skirt and pulled it back on and just kept going with the scene. The audience didn't laugh or anything. You should've been there."

"I don't really like plays," I say. "A bunch of people talking about nothing."

"Well, you would've liked this one. You should've heard Melissa after the play. She was so mad at the guy in charge of props, I thought she'd rip his face off. So what did you do today?"

"Still working on my bridge." I am connecting East Madham to West Madham with an eleven-foot-long suspension bridge. I've been working on it for months. It's really quite amazing.

"How's it going?"

"I've finally got the towers built." The entire bridge is scratch-built from matchsticks, string, and glue. Andy always teases me about that.

"Aren't you afraid it's gonna catch on fire?"

We laugh. Andy and I had some bad luck with fires when we were kids. We're more careful now. I always scrape the phosphorous tips off all the matchsticks before using them. I have scraped the heads off 112 boxes of stick matches. There are 200 matches in a box. In case you are slow at math, that's 22,400 matches in all.

"I figure the bridge will be ready for its inaugural crossing in about three weeks. Everybody in Madham will be there. You want to come?"

"Sure!"

Of course, the bit about "everybody in Madham" is kind of a joke, because the people who live in Madham are made out of plastic and they are less than one inch tall. Madham is the name of the HO scale railroad town I built in my basement. It covers three Ping-Pong tables and nearly fills the biggest room in the basement.

Madham has 109 buildings, all scratch-built. There are two lakes, a football stadium, a cement plant, a hospital, two tunnels, a forest, and sixty feet of track. It has a population of 289 plastic people, seventeen dogs, six cows, and eleven horses. Madham is the perfect town. In fact, one of my goals is to live in Madham. Once I figure out how to make a few million dollars, I'll build a full-scale version of the town with real trains and real trees and real people. I think it would be a nice place to live.

I've been working on Madham for two years and eleven months now. I guess you could say that I'm not only disturbed, I'm obsessed.

3

FOCUS

My ability to focus on one thing at a time is the secret to my success. Other people do not have this talent. Let me tell you: I once peeled an entire bag of tangerines—seventeen of them—using only my finger-nails, without losing one drop of juice. I lined up the peeled tangerines on the kitchen counter and they were as beautiful as any work of art. Mrs. Felko, my art teacher, would not agree with that. She and I have very different tastes. But I thought they were quite beautiful.

The special things I do are not always appreciated by my mother. She was upset about the tangerines. But

I still remember them: beautiful, naked, and soft orange, on green Formica.

I am like that with school assignments, too. That is, if the assignment interests me. I once was assigned to build a model windmill for science class. I made it out of Popsicle sticks, thread, wax paper, and copper wire. It actually worked. Math is also easy for me. It is all about focus and concentration. It is about doing exactly one thing at a time.

Andy understands the importance of focus. He knows how to focus when he is about to hit a golf ball, or when he is on stage in a play, or on the football field. Andy is a ferocious focuser. But he is not as good at it as I am. I can sit and watch a blade of grass grow. Andy, he can't do that for more than five minutes before he gets all itchy and has to get up and *do* something. Andy is a doer. Doing things is what he does.

One day—this was four years ago—Andy and I decided to build a tree house in Peanut Woods. We call it Peanut Woods because it's right behind the Skippy peanut butter factory, and it always smells like peanut butter.

Peanut Woods is not a very good woods. It's big enough—about sixteen acres in size—but the ground is squishy and swampy, and except for a few cottonwoods, there aren't a lot of big trees, and in the summer the mosquitoes can be ferocious. Andy and I used to go there when we were kids and build campfires. Andy was very good at fires. He never needed more than one match. Starting with a few scraps of paper, leaves, and slender twigs, he would slowly feed it larger twigs, then broken branches, then logs. The smoke kept the mosquitoes away. We would sit for hours, talking and watching the flames.

One big old cottonwood near the center of the woods was a perfect tree house tree—the trunk went straight up for twenty-five feet, then three huge branches spread out from a single bulbous crotch. We found a pile of old crates and pallets behind the Skippy factory. Andy borrowed a saw, a hammer, a couple of boxes of nails, and some nylon rope from his dad's workshop, and we went to work.

We started out by cutting steps from the pallets and nailing them to the trunk, three long nails per step. Once we made it up to the crotch, we set up a pulley system to haul the boards up the tree. Andy stayed up there sawing and nailing while I stayed below and fed him fresh lumber. Most of the time, however, I worked on carving our initials in the trunk:

A.M.
D.M.H.

It took me hours to carve those initials, but I did a remarkable job. I stripped off a rectangular section of bark, carefully outlined each letter with the tip of my pocketknife, then began to carve. I did not have a very good knife back then, just an old two-blade jackknife my father had given me, but I worked on those letters until each one was neat and straight and perfect. And all the while Andy was up there sawing and pounding and every now and then shouting, "Look out below!" when he was about to drop something.

It took us two days to build the tree house. It was three-sided, like a wedge of cheese, with a door in one wall, a window in each of the others, and a ceiling just high enough so we could stand up. We covered the floor with carpet samples. We found some wooden chairs and a table someone had thrown out. By the time we were done, it was just like a little triangle-shaped apartment.

The treehouse was a great place to hang out. Nobody knew about it but us.

A few months ago Andy and I visited the old cottonwood. The tree house is just a few charred, broken, rotting boards stuck way up in the branches. But you can still read our initials on the trunk, just as clear and precise as the day I carved them. Andy thinks that's funny—he worked a whole day building the tree house while I just carved our initials, but only the initials survived.

That is all you need to know about focus. If you take your time and do a job right, it can last forever.

4

LOGIC

My father owns seven identical gray suits, fifteen identical white dress shirts, three pairs of brown shoes, and twenty silk ties. Every tie is red and blue striped, but they are all different stripe patterns. Every year for his birthday I try to find a new variety of red-and-blue-striped silk tie. It can be quite challenging. One year I made a mistake and bought him a tie exactly like one he already owned, but he was very happy to get it because the old one had a coffee stain.

My father loves his suits. He even wears them on weekends. He wears a suit and tie to mow the lawn—although if it is really hot out, he will take off the jacket and roll up his shirtsleeves. Our neighbors find this strange, but many of their behaviors are also quite interesting. Mr. Ness, for example, likes to get drunk and play his electric guitar in his garage and sing old Rolling Stones songs. I find that very strange indeed.

Like me, my father is extremely intelligent. He is a professor at the university. He has written fourteen books about economics. You can actually go into a bookstore and see several of his books on the shelf. And by the way, he has a very good reason for always wearing a suit. He says that he has so many decisions to make in his work that he has no time to make decisions every day about trivial matters such as what he wears. He wears the same thing every day so he never has to think about it. It makes perfect sense when you think about it logically.

My father leaves the house at 7:08 every morning. He walks seven blocks to the bus stop, where he boards the number 14 bus, which delivers him almost to the door of Keyes Hall at the university. He does not drive his car to work. He says cars are wasteful and unnecessary. You might disagree with that, but I would advise you not to argue the point with my father.

One day I went to work with him and watched what he did all day. I listened to him lecture about economics. It was highly enlightening. One thing that surprised me was how energetic and happy he seemed while he was lecturing. He even made some funny jokes, which he never does at home.

My father is normally very quiet and polite—as long as you don't argue with him. If you argue with him, he becomes very loud. He has been known to shout. Every now and then he will have a disagreement with my mother. He makes his case in a highly logical and mostly indisputable fashion. For instance, a couple of months ago they disagreed about buying a new sofa. My father was against it. He presented his argument, his voice increasing in volume with each point.

"We do not *need* a new sofa, Andrea. First, our *existing* sofa is perfectly adequate. It is both comfortable and attractive. Second, a new sofa would *cost several hundred dollars*—OR MORE! Our financial resources are finite. Third, by DISCARDING the EXISTING sofa, we would be contributing to the EVER-INCREASING MASS OF HUMAN WASTE PRODUCTS THAT IS TAKING OVER THE SURFACE OF OUR PLANET! Furthermore, **I SEE NO REASON WHY WE SHOULD HAVE TO GO TO THE TIME AND TROUBLE TO GET USED TO A NEW PIECE OF FURNITURE THAT WE DO NOT NEED!**"

By the time he delivered that last line, he was red-faced and pounding his left palm with his right fist.

My mother is used to my father's hyperlogical rages. She simply smiled and said, "I understand, dear."

The next afternoon, while my father was at work, a truck from Wickes Furniture arrived at our house. Two men carried a new sofa into our living room. They removed the old sofa and added it to the ever-increasing mass of human waste products that is taking over the surface of our planet.

That night when my father arrived home, he walked

right past the new sofa without seeming to notice anything different. In fact, he hasn't said a word about the sofa since. Maybe he is choosing to ignore it, or maybe he is simply oblivious. Either way, I'm sure he has a very logical reason for his position.

5

SECRETS

Best friends have secrets. Andy and I are no exception. Of course, I can't really discuss all of our secrets, because if I did they would not be secrets anymore. But I can tell about this one thing, because we got caught and so it is a secret no more. It is an *ex*-secret.

The secret I'm talking about, the secret that isn't a secret anymore, has to do with the Tuttle place on Redbud Road. Mrs. Tuttle, who was ninety-six years old at the time, died a few years ago. Andy and I were thirteen. After she died, her son Jack cleaned out her house and put up a FOR SALE sign. Every now and then somebody would look at the house, but it had so many problems that no one wanted to buy it. The roof was rotten, the foundation was collapsing, the plumbing was rusted and leaky, and there were bats in the attic. Also, it was way down at the end of Redbud Road, with no other houses in sight.

The Tuttle place had been for sale for almost a year the day Andy and I broke in.

It was a chilly, breezy early spring afternoon. Andy and I were out walking and talking the way we always did. I was wearing a light windbreaker, and I was cold. We were walking by the Tuttle place when Andy noticed a window that hadn't been closed all the way.

"Let's go in and check it out," he said. Or maybe it was me who said it. Actually, I'm pretty sure it was me.

We climbed in through the window. It was warmer inside. The sun was slanting in hard through the windows. The rooms were bright and clean and empty. Jack Tuttle had gotten rid of almost all the furniture, refinished the wood floors to a pale golden yellow, and painted all the walls bright white. I guess he thought maybe people would overlook the roof and the plumbing if the paint was fresh.

Andy and I wandered through the echoey spaces, a forbidden kingdom, clean and white and separate from the world. After we explored the whole house, we sat down in the middle of the biggest room in the house and talked for hours. While we talked, I carved a design in the maple floor next to the big stone fireplace. When Andy and I find a place that is important to us, we like to leave our mark. Maple is very hard wood, and difficult to carve, but I am very focused, and I always finish what I start.

The design I carved that afternoon is gone now, but I still remember its lines and curves as if I carved it yesterday. I had been working on it in my head for a long time. It became our sign, our secret mark, our sigil:

In case you can't see it for yourself, the design contains Andy's and my initials. Still can't see it? Here's what they look like separated:

And here are the parts they have in common:

Can you see it? It looks like two people sitting at a campfire. Me and Andy. I'm the one on the left because I have a low body temperature and I like to sit closer to the flames.

Anyway, as I mentioned, as far as the Tuttle place goes, our secret didn't last.

But I don't really feel like talking about that right now.

6

TROUBLED

Do I strike you as troubled?

Let me give you some facts and figures. I am seventeen years old. I am a junior at Fairview Central. I have never skipped school and I have a 3.4 grade point average. I do not use drugs or alcohol. I have never been seriously ill. I have never broken a bone, lost a limb, or had an organ removed. I am scrupulously honest, except for necessary lies. I sleep well at night. I am not a loner. I have a best friend.

According to an article I read, 17 percent of all boys between the ages of twelve and twenty are "troubled." By this they mean that 17 percent of us have psychological or behavioral aberrations that may pose a threat to others or to ourselves. In my opinion, 17 percent is far too low an estimate. To be accurate you would have to include the entire football team (except for Andy), all of the stoners, the dropouts, the gear heads, the art students, and at least half of the chess club. According to my data, about 38 percent of the Fairview student body is "troubled," or if they are not, they should be.

I do not include myself in their number.

The reason I am going on about this is because one night I overheard my mother talking to my father:

"Henry, I'm worried about Douglas."

"What's the boy done now?"

"Well, the fact that he spends hours every night working on his model railroad . . ."

"He enjoys it, Andrea. A boy has to have a hobby."

"Yes, but he spends *so* much time at it. I think that town is almost *real* to him."

"You must admit, it is quite realistic. Remarkable, actually."

"I just wish he would get out more. Spend more time with other kids his age."

"He's shy. I was a shy boy too. He'll learn to make friends as he gets older."

"Nevertheless, I am concerned. I heard him talking in his room again last night."

"What was he saying?"

"I don't know, but that can't be normal, can it?"

"I used to talk to myself when I was a boy. It's just a phase."

"I just don't think Dr. Ahlstrom is helping him."

"The boy seems happy enough."

"Happy children do not talk to themselves, dear."

I find it curious that my parents, both of whom are extremely intelligent, don't realize that the voices my mother heard were me and Andy. I mean, we've been talking across the picket fence for years. You'd have to be pretty oblivious to not figure it out. And as far as spending too much time working on my model railroad goes, all I can say is, it isn't half as nuts as some of the stuff she does.

My mother has more facts and figures packed inside her head than anyone I know. She can name the fifty highest mountain peaks in the world, in order, and tell you how high they are. She knows the atomic weight of every element, and she can tell you what "syzygy" means. Her job, which she does at home in her office, is designing crossword puzzles. You may have seen her work in the *New York Times* and other important publications.

But I have seen her spend an hour searching the house for her reading glasses when they were on a chain around her neck the whole time. I have also seen her throw a fit over a broken pencil lead. And then there was the time she was trying to roast a chicken and accidentally put the chicken in the bread drawer and a loaf of plastic-wrapped bread in the oven. That stank up the house pretty good.

I could come up with several other examples for both of my parents, but my point is that sometimes even a highly intelligent person can be dumb as a stump.

7

PRACTICE

I have an appointment to see Dr. Eleanor Ahlstrom every Thursday after school. Dr. Ahlstrom is nearly as intelligent as my parents and far more interesting to talk to. But I agree with my mother about one thing: Dr. Ahlstrom is not helping me one bit. Why? Because I do not need help—it's as simple as that.

So this Thursday I do something I have never done before. I skip my appointment with Dr. Ahlstrom. Instead, I go to the athletic field and sit on the highest tier and watch the football practice.

At first I can't pick Andy out of the confused mass of blue and yellow. I know he is a quarterback, but today they are doing running drills. Finally I see him, number 17, his long legs pumping as he dodges and twists and snakes his way gracefully through the defensive line.

After the practice I wait outside the school for him to come out. He's in there a long time. All the other guys on the team come out and get into their cars or take off walking, but no Andy. Maybe he left by another entrance. I start walking home, but I've only gone a few yards when I hear him call my name.

"Dougie! Wait up!"

I look back, and see Andy running after me.

"Hey," I say.

"Hey. I saw you up in the stands."

"I thought you might have."

"What's going on?"

"Nothing. I just decided to skip Ahlstrom today."

"I don't blame you."

"I still don't get why they make me see a counselor and not you."

"I don't have time," Andy says. "With football and theater and stuff. I guess my folks think if I stay busy all the time, I won't get in trouble."

"Too busy to be *disturbed*."

"I guess." He looks at me and grins and says, "Hey, you want to hit the BK?"

Which was exactly what I hoped he'd say.

Andy and I have a running debate over whether Burger King fries are better than McDonald's fries. I myself prefer the BK fries because they are crispier, but Andy likes McDonald's fries for their extra-fatty flavor. But we both agree that BK makes a superior burger, so that's where we usually end up.

We order our usual mess of food. I pay for it. Andy is always broke. But that's okay. I have money. My grandfather not only left me his train set, he left me an allowance of one hundred dollars a month. Most of it I spend on model trains, but I usually have some left over for other important things, like junk food. We take our food to the booth in the back and start stuffing our faces and talking. Andy tells me more details about the play he is in, *A Streetcar Named Desire*. He tells me the whole story, and even though I know the story already (I once saw the movie version on TV), I listen to him, because that is what best friends do. Then I tell him about a mistake I found in the calculus text, and we talk about Melissa Haverman for a while.

"You should ask her out," I say.

"She's not my type."

"I'd ask her out if I was you."

"Then why don't *you* ask her out?"

"Why don't you shut UP!" I stuff another handful of fries in my mouth. I hate when Andy turns things around on me. He knows I could never ask out a girl like Melissa. In fact, the whole dating thing seems like so much trouble, I am thinking I might just skip it altogether. Actually, the idea of being a loner appeals to me.

Andy is looking at me, making me feel guilty for yelling at him. *He* should feel guilty. After we are done eating, we walk home, talking about some ideas I have for Madham. Then Andy asks me if I'm going to the football game Friday night.

"I'm starting quarterback," he says.

"You're always starting quarterback."

"So you gonna come?"

"I don't think so. I have to work on the bridge."

"You should get out more."

"That's what my mom says."

Neither of us brings up Melissa again. That is the secret to staying best friends with someone—you learn what not to talk about. For instance, we never talk about the Tuttle place. We don't like to think about that.

8

WORM

Melissa Haverman's blond hair is as fine and soft as a cat's fur. Her skin is smooth and pale, her eyes are green and gold, and her lips are shaped exactly like how you would imagine a perfect pair of lips to be shaped. She is also fairly intelligent. On a scale of one to ten, Melissa Haverman is a nine point seven. The only thing that prevents her from being a perfect ten is that she thinks I am a disgusting troll.

Sitting in calculus, first period, I am listening with 10 percent of my brain to Mr. Kesselbaum's stony voice and devoting the rest of my mind to observing Melissa Haverman. She is sitting two rows over. If I lean forward a little, I have a clear view of her. Exceptionally clear. We are on the east side of the building, and the sun comes in so strong that Mr. Kesselbaum has to close the blinds. But they don't quite close all the way. A bright bar of sunlight slips in under them and glances off the aluminum sill and lights up Melissa's profile. I can see the soft, downy fuzz close to her skin.

Have I mentioned how good my eyes are? I have amazingly good eyes. I could count the hairs on a fly's legs from across the room. Okay, maybe not. But I can see. I can see her eyelashes, each separate and distinct. She is watching Mr. Kesselbaum, her brow slightly furrowed, her green-nailed hand holding a pen poised over a notebook page. She is a good, attentive student. I respect that. I wonder if she respects me. I mean, I know she thinks I'm a disgusting troll, but she might still respect me for my intelligence.

I imagine us trapped together. Caught in a Force 5 tornado. Trapped in the basement of a collapsed building. Just me and Melissa. Melissa is unconscious. Her sweater and jeans have been badly torn, and she has tiny cuts all over her body from flying shards of glass. I find a first aid kit and gently, lovingly, tend to her wounds. . . .

"Mr. Kesselbaum!" Melissa's hand is in the air.

"Yes, Melissa?"

"Would you please ask Dougie to stop staring at me?"

All eyes are on me now.

Mr. Kesselbaum shakes his head wearily. "Douglas . . . if you must ogle, please ogle me."

"I wasn't ogling," I say.

"In any case, it would behoove you to keep your eyes on the front of the room."

"Yes, sir," I say. I am always very polite. A few seconds later I sneak a look at Melissa and catch *her* staring at *me*. Her eyes narrow and her lips curl to form a silent word.

I'm pretty sure the word is "worm."

9

RAT

Friday night things get tense at the Hanson residence when Andrea Doris Louis-Hanson tells Henry Clay Hanson that their son, Douglas MacArthur Hanson, failed to keep his appointment with Dr. Eleanor Ahlstrom. Words are exchanged. Accusations fly. Ignorance and delusion are revealed, naked and ugly. Threats burn up the air like wildfire. Concessions are displayed and offered for sale. Promises are surgically extracted. I end up in my room. I am quite worried about my parents. Some of the theories my father advanced were quite bizarre, and my mother seemed to accept them. I think they are both losing touch with reality.

I spread myself out on my bed and search my mind for a peaceful place to be. I find a cozy clearing in the woods outside of Madham. I am sitting before a campfire. I move close to the flames and let them warm me. That lasts for only a few minutes. I am distracted by a knotted sensation deep in my gut. I worry that I might have a blood clot in my hepatic vein. I have heard of this happening. The hepatic vein carries blood away from the liver. Blockage can lead to a painful death. I do not want to die painfully.

There are many ways to die, and most of them are pretty bad. When Andy and I were little kids, we used to argue about it.

"Would you rather burn to death or freeze to death?"

"Freeze, for sure," Andy said. "Fire hurts too much."

"But it's faster."

"Yeah, but when you freeze you just get numb and then you fall asleep."

"I don't like to be cold."

The thought of freezing to death still makes me shiver.

A few years ago I read about some Buddhist monks who poured gasoline over themselves and set themselves on fire. They did it to protest a war. The article quoted a doctor who claimed that the burning monks experienced little pain.

"They quickly go into shock," said the doctor. "I don't think they feel a thing after the first few seconds."

This supports my preference for fire over ice. In fact, since I showed him the article, Andy has come around to my point of view.

I sit up in bed and put my feet on the floor. The

throbbing from my hepatic vein fades. Maybe I'm not about to die after all. I go to the window and look across the fence at Andy's window. It's dark and the blinds are closed. Andy must not be home. Of course he's not home—it's Friday night.

Andy is playing football.

I think of myself as a shadow, skirting the perimeter of the stadium. Actually, it is just a football field with twelve tiers of bleachers running down each side, surrounded by a chain-link fence. I blend in with the blacks and grays, circling the colorful house of games, listening to the shouts and cheers. I pause at one corner of the field where I can see through the chain-link fence between the stands. Metal halide lamps blast photons onto a bright green grass rectangle. Little men in costume run and crash into one another, our home team, the Hornets, in blue and yellow, the other team in red and white. All primary colors represented.

The stands are mostly empty; only about two hundred spectators have showed up, most of them clustered at the fifty yard line. There is room for ten times that many, but the only time the stadium fills up is for the homecoming game, and that was last week. I hope Andy isn't disappointed in tonight's crowd.

I watch through the fence for about twelve minutes, but I am frustrated by the poor view. I could buy a ticket, but I would have to pay full price for a game that is more than half over. I look left, I look right, I look up. I shift into ninja mode and plunge my fingers into the chain-link and scramble up and over, dropping catlike into the carefully guarded compound, unobserved. I walk non-chalantly between the stands, then climb up to the top tier at the seventeen yard line and sit. No one notices me.

I watch the game carefully for a few minutes. The other team has the ball, so Andy is on the bench, but I can't pick him out of the cluster of blue and yellow Hornets. Bored, I look down between my feet. I can see the ground beneath the stands. It is littered with paper cups and hot dog trays and candy wrappers and all sorts of other junk. They still haven't cleaned up the mess from last week's homecoming game.

The crowd roars; I look up and see a Hornet running hard. He disappears into a mass of red and white on the twenty yard line. Somehow the Hornets have intercepted the ball. They send their offensive line out onto the field, where they form a huddle. The huddle breaks; number seventeen—that's Andy—takes a stance close behind the center. Sudden movement, Andy has the ball, he's backing up, he throws a perfect pass . . . but the ball slips from the receiver's hands.

I look down, disappointed. The litter below is stirring. At first I think its the wind, but then I see a small dark shape scurry off with something white in its mouth. A rat. I shudder, remembering another conversation Andy and I had about death: Would you rather be strangled by a serial killer or devoured by rats? As I recall, we both went with the serial killer.

I watch for a time, but the rat does not return. I hear a groan from the crowd. When I look up, the red and white team has the ball. I shift my attention to the crowd, trying to pick out individual faces. I see Aron Wiseman's bushy red hair. I see Gracie Monroe—she's easy to pick out because she weighs about three hundred pounds and dresses in purple. I recognize several other students and a couple of teachers. And I see a blond girl that might or might not be Melissa Haverman. I focus my eyes on her, staring hard. Finally she turns her head so that the light hits her face and I see that it is another girl, one I do not know.

I look down. The rat is back, his head in a discarded popcorn cup. I can see his naked tail. He backs out of the cup holding a popped kernel in his mouth and scurries off through the litter.

My hands are getting cold. I bury them in my pockets and feel several hard sticklike objects. Farmer matches. Like the ones I've been scraping the heads off of so I can use the sticks to build my suspension bridge. The matches in my pocket still have their heads, red and white, strike anywhere. I take one from my pocket and hold its white tip against the rough wood of the bleacher and wait, counting. At 348 seconds the rat returns right on schedule. I wait until his head is deep inside the popcorn cup, then strike the match and drop it. The flaming match lands three inches away from the cup. The rat leaps straight up, sending the cup and popcorn flying, and hits the ground running. I am laughing.

The match continues to burn. It is only a few millimeters away from a crumpled napkin. I watch until the match burns out. A wisp of back smoke curls upward and disappears, and all is still.

I watch and count. I count to five hundred, but the rat does not return.

The litter below me takes on an evil taint, and I

become angry with the nameless, faceless people whose job it is to clean beneath the stands. I am thinking about rats and the bubonic plague. Garbage-eating rats covered with lice and fleas and bacteria. I saw only one rat, but there are probably hundreds of them feeding off the popcorn and chips and half-eaten hot dogs. Rats multiplying and spreading disease and filth. Rats in the school. Rats nosing around our homes in the night, searching for a crevice large enough to wriggle through.

I light another match and drop it. It hits a patch of bare dirt and goes out. I try again and get one to land right in a mustard-smeared hot dog tray, but it only burns for three seconds. I count the remaining matches. Fourteen.

The crowd roars; I look up to see a Hornet dancing in the end zone, holding the ball high. It is number seventeen. Andy has made a touchdown. I hold seven matches together and strike them and drop them into the litter. Five of them go out on impact, one gets caught in a bleacher support and burns out against the steel, and one burns for a full ten seconds, the flame licking at the side of a soda cup, then dies. The crowd groans; the Hornets have missed kicking their extra point.

I go back to lighting matches one at a time. I manage to land the last match on a napkin that puffs into a bright yellow flame, but the only thing touching the napkin is a waxy soda cup that refuses to ignite.

Oh, well. Rats, cockroaches, and vultures will inherit the earth. The Hornets are ahead twenty-three to six. Twenty-three minus six is seventeen. It is seventeen minutes before ten o'clock.

I am out of matches. Time to go home.

10

BUTTERFINGERS

The last time Andy and I climbed the old cottonwood to our tree house was the second winter after we built it, eight days before Christmas. A foot and a half of light snow had fallen the night before. We were up to our knees in it.

The woods are a different place after a heavy snow. The paths disappear, and the low brush is hidden. Tree branches are topped with tall ridges of snow, the rough trunks spotted and veined with white.

It is very quiet. If you stand perfectly still, you can hear the clumps fall from the trees and strike the soft, sparkly surface with a soft *whuff*.

Andy and I had brought presents for each other.

Another eight days seemed like too long to wait, so we went to the tree house to celebrate our own private Christmas. I had bought Andy a giant bag of Butterfingers. They were in an old shoe box wrapped in the Sunday comic section, the closest thing I had to real wrapping paper. Butterfingers were Andy's favorite candy. They were my favorite too. I was hoping he might share them with me.

It took us a while to find the big cottonwood. Everything looked so different, and the deep snow was full of surprises: invisible logs and holes and branches to trip over. The ground beneath the snow was still squishy and unfrozen. At one point Andy stepped into a sinkhole and went in up to his knee. When he pulled his leg out it was completely soaked and his boot was covered with muck. He laughed and kept on walking.

We finally found the cottonwood. Andy quickly climbed the steps up to the tree house. I shoved Andy's present into my jacket and followed, testing each step carefully. The nails were more than a year old, and some of the steps wiggled alarmingly. I never liked climbing that tree. Andy outweighed me by a good twenty pounds, so I knew the steps would hold me, but I still didn't like the climb.

Inside, the tree house was dry and cold. A pile of seeds had appeared in one corner, probably stashed there by a squirrel. We threw out the seeds, brushed the snow from the window ledges, and shook out the carpet samples that covered the floor.

"We should get one of those portable heaters," Andy said.

"There's no place to plug it in."

"We could get a really long extension cord."

"Or we could get a kerosene heater."

"How about an air conditioner for the summer?"

"And a TV."

"And an elevator, so you don't have to climb those steps."

"I hate those steps."

Andy laughed. "Oh well." He pulled a small gift-wrapped package from his jacket pocket. "Merry Christmas, Dougie."

I opened that package in about two seconds, and when I saw what it was, I felt incredibly good and incredibly awful all at once.

"Andy . . . it's—wow—it's really nice."

"I knew you'd like it."

I turned the knife in my hands, admiring the smooth, hard red case. "An Explorer," I said. "Victorinox Explorer. Wow."

"It has seventeen tools. That's your number, right?"

"Yeah." I unfolded the knife blade, the scissors, the screwdriver, the magnifying glass. . . . "It must have cost you a fortune." In fact, I knew exactly how much the Swiss Army knife went for: $44.90 plus tax at Pike's Hardware. Twelve times as much as I'd paid for the bag of Butterfingers.

Andy shrugged. "I got a deal on it. Pike traded it to me for cleaning out his basement."

I folded the tools back into the knife and squeezed it in my fist. "It's heavy," I said. "It feels really solid."

Andy was grinning, enjoying the moment. I opened

the small knife blade and began to carve the date on the wall. Andy watched me for a few minutes, then asked, "What's in the box?"

"Huh?"

"That box you've got." He pointed at the shoe box with the Butterfingers inside.

"Oh. Um . . . it's for you." I pushed it toward him, then watched him peel away the paper and pull the top off.

His eyes opened wide and he said, "Oh, man, my favorite!" He tore open the bag of candy. "You got me the big size! Awesome!" He ripped into a Butterfinger and took a huge bite, rolling his eyes with pleasure as he crunched away. "I love these things," he said, his mouth full of gold and brown candy.

"It's not as nice as what you gave me," I said.

"Are you kidding? You can't eat that knife, can you? Here!" He thrust the bag at me, and I took a Butterfinger for myself.

I'm making a short story long. The point is, Andy is the one who gave me the Victorinox Explorer seventeen-tool Swiss Army knife that later on got us in so much trouble. But what I really wanted to tell you is why it was the last time we ever climbed up that old cottonwood.

11

TO BUILD A FIRE

It was quite cold that day, and Andy's right leg was soaked with ice-cold water from stepping in the sinkhole. We each ate a couple Butterfingers, which helped me feel not so guilty, but it didn't really warm us up much. Andy was pretty miserable with his wet foot, so I suggested that we make a little campfire right there on the floor of the tree house.

"You can't have a fire in a tree house," Andy said. "It's made out of wood. It'll burn."

"Not if we make a ring of snow around it."

"The snow will just melt."

"Yeah, and the floor will get wet so it can't burn.

And if it gets out of control, we can just throw more snow on it."

Andy wasn't so sure about that, but I can be very convincing. My position was highly logical, and it is hard to argue with logic.

We climbed down the tree and gathered some dry twigs and branches and carried them back up to the tree house and piled them in the middle of the floor. We scooped a few armloads of snow off the roof and packed it into a ring around the wood, then stuffed some candy wrappers and the Sunday comic section into the twigs.

"I don't know about this," Andy said.

"It'll be okay," I said, pulling a book of matches from my jacket pocket. You never know when you might need a fire. One of my all-time favorite stories is *To Build a Fire* by Jack London. A man in the Arctic wilderness falls through the ice into a stream and gets his legs soaked. He has to build a fire fast or he will freeze to death. I won't tell you what happens in the end, but it is very interesting.

I lit the fire.

At first it was very exciting because the Butterfinger wrappers burned fast and flaming bits of paper floated up and started landing where they shouldn't. We quickly stomped them out, and the fire settled down and started to behave itself. Once it calmed down, Andy took off his wet boot and sock and put his foot near the fire.

"That feels good," he said.

After a few minutes it started to get pretty smoky. Some of it went out the windows and door, but most of the smoke wanted to hang around. As long as we kept our faces close to the floor we were okay. Andy stretched out on his back, toasting his foot like a marshmallow. He was on his third Butterfinger.

"Y'know, the Butterfingers are just my first present for you," I said. "I'm going to get you something else. Something really nice."

"You don't have to."

"Yeah, but I'm gonna. Maybe I'll buy you a motor-cycle."

"If you get me a motorcycle, I'll buy you a car."

"I'll buy you a tank."

"Then I'll have to get you an F-sixteen."

"I'd rather have a stealth bomber."

"How about a space shuttle?"

The room was so full of smoke that we couldn't see the ceiling. It was like being under a low cloud. The tops of the flames disappeared into gray murk.

It was Andy who first noticed how hot the floor was getting.

"It feels good, doesn't it?" I said.

"I don't know. . . ." Andy crawled to the door and hung his head out. "Hey, Dougie, I think we better get out of here."

"Why? It's not that smoky."

"C'mere and look underneath us."

I crawled over next to him—the floor was getting really hot—and stuck my head out and looked at the underside of the tree house and saw a sheet of flame. The underside of the floor was completely on fire.

"Come on!" Andy was out the door, his feet on the top step. I started after him, then remembered I'd left my knife stuck in the wall.

"Wait—my knife!" I crawled back inside where the fire was suddenly roaring and groped for my Swiss Army knife. I was blind from the smoke when I finally felt the smooth plastic handle hit my palm. I felt my way back to the door, choking and coughing, my palms blistering, and went out headfirst, forgetting that I was thirty feet up a tree.

Andy caught me. I don't know how he did it, or how that top step held under our combined weight, but somehow his arm was around me and I slammed into the trunk and the burning floor fell out of the tree house and crashed, hissing, into the snow. We climbed shakily down the steps and stood there watching as the rest of the tree house went up in flames.

I looked at Andy, who was standing on one leg, holding his bare foot up out of the snow.

"Well," I said, "you were right."

"My Butterfingers must be all melted," he said.

"I'll get you another bag."

He looked down at his bare foot. "How am I gonna walk out of here?"

I took off my stocking cap and we used the string from his parka hood to tie it around his ankle. It wasn't the best boot, but it helped. By the time we got home, his toes and my ears were frostbit, and I had blisters all over my palms. But it wasn't so bad. The cottonwood itself didn't burn up, I still had my Swiss Army knife, and we didn't get into trouble. I washed my own smoky-smelling clothes and bandaged my own hands. I told my mother that I had fallen down and scraped my palms on the sidewalk. My mother is extremely intelligent, but for some reason she believed me. I bought Andy another bag of Butterfingers, and I also bought him a pair of battery-powered electric socks.

It's become a tradition with us. Every year I buy him a brand-new pair of electric socks. I don't want him to ever have cold feet again.

12

SIGIL

You might get the idea that Andy and I have an unhealthy relationship with fire, but you would be wrong. Fire is simply a tool to be used responsibly, like a hammer or a car or a train. We never start a fire just to watch something burn. We use it to accomplish definite goals, like to stay warm.

For example, we started the fire in the tree house for a very important purpose. Andy's foot was cold and wet, and we had to do something about it. True, the fire did not work out as planned, but sometimes you just can't control the way things go. What happened at the Tuttle place was another example of that. And that's all I have to say about *that*.

Although art is my worst subject at school, I do not hate it. In fact, I am quite interested in lettering. I have been working on the sigil. The idea of combining our initials into one symbolic design started back at the Tuttle place. A few weeks after that, I added serifs to the letters and came up with a more refined version:

Since then I have been using my time in art class to improve the design. Mrs. Felko is quite patient with me, although she is constantly telling me to "draw from the heart."

"I *am* drawing from the heart," I say.

"You could liven up your lines, Douglas. Hold the pen loosely, let your hand talk to the paper."

Like many of my teachers, Mrs. Felko is completely insane.

What I enjoy doing is changing my design one parameter at a time. For instance, I recently completed an outline version that I find quite interesting:

I think it looks like an ancient Celtic rune or maybe the logo of a corporation run by elves. I am working now on one in yellow and blue, our school colors. I am planning to give it to Andy to hang on his wall.

The sigil is an expression of my theory about focus. I have found that doing one thing over and over for a long period of time can be extremely satisfying. I try to explain this to Mrs. Felko.

"That's all very well, Douglas, but what we are doing here in this class is learning how to do new things. Everyone else in class is working on their clay sculptures, and here you are, painting your symbol."

"It's not a symbol. It's a sigil."

"Well, I want you to put your 'sigil' away for now and get yourself some clay and try something new."

"Yes, Mrs. Felko," I say politely. So I scoop some clay from the plastic bin at the back of the room and use a rolling pin to flatten it into a slab about one inch thick. I then trace the outline of the sigil on its surface and begin to carve. A few minutes later, Mrs. Felko stops by to see how I am doing. The sound of her sigh is like air rushing out of a punctured balloon.

"Well, Douglas, I see you have found your muse."

"What does that mean?"

She shakes her head. "Are you ever going to share with us the meaning of that device?"

"It's not a device, it's a sigil."

"I see," she said. Although it is perfectly clear to me that she does not understand a thing.

13

I SPY

Melissa Haverman lives at 3417 Oak View Terrace in the Woodland Trails development. Her house has lots of big windows and a wraparound second-story deck, and it is located on a large lot surrounded by trees. All the Woodland Trails lots are surrounded by trees. The idea is that every house in the development is separated from its neighbors by a "greenway," or a belt of trees about fifty feet wide. That way they can pretend they are living in the middle of a great forest. I've seen the sales brochures: *In the Arms of Nature—Safe, Forested Privacy Only 20 Minutes from Downtown.*

Of course, the privacy is an illusion. They are still

close enough to hear one another's lawn mowers. The safety is an illusion too. Anybody could be hiding in the greenway—criminals, escapees from the insane asylum, or serial killers.

Or me. I am sitting in the crotch of an oak tree looking into Melissa Haverman's bedroom. I guess that is why they call her street Oak View Terrace. It is eleven o'clock at night, but Melissa has not yet gone to bed. Her room is dark except for the faint yellow glow of a night-light.

I suspect that she is downstairs watching television. I wonder how late her parents will let her stay up.

Time passes, which I measure in seventeen-second intervals: 17, 34, 51, 68, 85, 102, 119, 136, 153, 170, 187. . . . I once counted as high as 78,251 before being interrupted. I am always getting interrupted, which is the main challenge to staying focused. My goal is to count to 170,000 by 17s. To do that I would probably have to hide in a cave or something.

I am at 9,520 when the light goes on in Melissa's room.

She is wearing a pink sweatshirt and blue jeans and her hair is tied back in a ponytail. She closes the door and kicks off her shoes and throws herself back on her bed. For thirty-four seconds she just lays there perfectly still, then she sits up and takes off her sweatshirt. She is wearing a white tank top underneath. She stands and carefully folds the sweatshirt and walks it to the part of her room I can't see. She is out of sight for almost a minute, then she reappears, still wearing the same jeans and tank top, but with her hair loose. She stops right in front of the window and stares out, directly at me. She can't really be seeing me. She must be looking at her reflection in the glass. I know I am invisible to her in my dark and leafy nest, but the feeling is quite eerie. I am holding my breath.

Her mouth moves. Who is she talking to? She gestures with one hand, a dismissive, "what*ever*" flick of the wrist, then she laughs and her mouth forms the words "No way."

Is she talking to her reflection? Then I see the thin black cord trailing from her soft blond hair, and I notice the cell phone clipped to the waistband of her jeans. She is talking on her headset. She laughs again and her mouth twists into a disgusted grimace and I can make out the word she is mouthing as clearly as if she were whispering it into my ear: *"Worm."*

The tree starts to spin and I realize that I am still holding my breath. I let it out and replace the dead air in my lungs with fresh oxygen.

Melissa has her back to the window now and is waving her hands; she is doing a little dance, wiggling her butt and shaking her hair. Then she stops and removes the headset and unclips the phone from her jeans. She starts to unbutton her jeans, then stops, walks a few steps to the window and stares out into the darkness.

I am crawling back into my bedroom through the window when I hear Andy say, "You're gonna get caught."

I see his white grin in his dark window.

"Not if you keep your voice down," I whisper.

"I don't mean here and now. I mean over in Woodland. Spying on Melissa."

"How did you know where I was?"

"Where else would you be at midnight on a Monday night?"

"Maybe I was just taking a walk."

"Yeah, a walk to Woodland Trails."

"A guy has to walk someplace."

"You're gonna get caught."

"I stayed in the greenway. Nobody could see me."

"I'm telling you."

"I was careful."

"So, how is she?"

"She's . . . fine."

"You talk to her?"

"No! I just . . . I watched her get ready for bed."

"Really? How ready? You see her blue panties?"

"She took off her sweatshirt. She had on a tank top underneath."

"Then what?"

"Then she closed the shades."

"Just like last time."

"Yeah."

"Just like every time."

"I don't know why. I mean, the whole point of living there is the privacy. Who does she think is going to be looking?"

"Well, there's you."

"She doesn't know that."

"Why don't you just ask her out? I mean, you know so much about her. How could she say no?"

"Shut up." I turn my back on him and crawl through the window and close it behind me, but I can still see his grin, floating in the dark.

14

BRIDGE

The Madham suspension bridge is based upon the Golden Gate Bridge, which I once crossed at the age of six years and four months in a car with my parents. Of course, my model is much smaller than the original. In fact, it is a 1:800 scale model.

As you may know, HO gauge trains are 1:87 models of the real thing, so when I finish the bridge, the train will just barely fit between the uprights. Relatively speaking, if a train that size went across the real Golden Gate Bridge it would be 120 feet tall.

You may wonder why I didn't build the bridge to HO scale. The reason is because it would have had to be more than one hundred feet long. It would not have fit in the basement. I might be troubled, I might be disturbed, I might be obsessed—but I'm not crazy.

There are five critical elements in a suspension bridge: the uprights, the anchors, the deck, the cables, and the stringers. Each element must be brought into perfect balance with each of the other four elements. If one element is too weak, the entire structure collapses.

The towers and deck of my bridge are built of strike-anywhere matches with the heads scraped off. I do not want my bridge to spontaneously combust. I carefully scrape away all traces of phosphorus, leaving a fifty-four-millimeter-long matchstick. For the suspension cables I use orange braided nylon cord, and for the stringers I use cotton string, which I dye orange using Rit dye. Many people do not know this, but the Golden Gate Bridge is not actually golden. It is a color called International Orange.

I have been working on the bridge for several months. It is now only a few weeks away from completion. Opening Day will be November 17. I've invited Andy to join me as I send a seventeen-car train across the bridge for the first time. Andy understands about me and bridges. Not everyone else is smart enough to get it.

For example, here is what Mr. Haughton, my language arts teacher, said about bridges during the midquarter evaluation:

"Douglas, I can see that you are passionate about your subject matter. Passion is very important to a writer. But maybe you could try to write on another topic?"

"I could write something about the original Golden Gate Bridge."

"I was thinking you might write about something other than bridges."

"Why?"

Mr. Haughton sat back in his chair and stroked his chin. It was the first time I ever saw someone do that except in a movie.

"Douglas, Douglas, Douglas . . . ," he said to give himself time to think. "Let me try to explain. . . ." Mr. Haughton can be ponderous at times. "The writer is like a bridge builder. When you set words down on paper, you are building a bridge between yourself and the reader. And if what you write fails to engage the reader, your effort has been in vain. You have built a bridge to nowhere. Do you understand what I am saying?"

"The writer is like a bridge builder."

"Yes. The bridges you build are, in fact, deliberate acts of communication. But if what you are writing is not *interesting,* then you have wasted your time. Do you understand?"

"You don't find bridges interesting."

"Yes. I mean no. The problem is not with bridges *per se.* It is the fact that you describe your model bridge in such excruciating detail, with so much repetition, with so many measurements and formulas and numbers . . . the fact is, very few readers will be able to follow your thoughts."

"Do you think I need to explain more?"

"No!" He almost shouted the word, then closed his eyes and took a deep breath. "Douglas, I just think that if you were to write on a topic that was not so . . . *important* to you, your writing might in fact be clearer and more readable. As a related comment on your work, I'd like to remind you that when I ask for a three page essay, it is not necessary for you to turn in a thirty page dissertation."

"Some of those pages were drawings and photographs."

"Yes, well, even so, you must have had five thousand words in there."

"Four thousand nine hundred thirteen." That's seventeen cubed, but I don't bother pointing that out to Mr. Haughton. "You said that we could write a longer essay for extra credit."

"I did? Oh, well, perhaps I did . . . but in the future, Douglas . . . please consider another topic. That's all I'm saying."

As you can see, Mr. Haughton is not a clear-thinking individual. What he says actually makes little sense. Consider the following useful information that Mr. Haughton wanted me to cut out of my essay:

Total length of bridge: 3.33 meters. Length of main span: 2.34 meters. Width of bridge: 7 cm. Clearance above water: 12 cm. Height of towers: 34 cm. Number of main cables: 2. Composition of main cables: braided 1/4-inch nylon cord (orange). Number of stringers: 391. Composition of stringers: cotton string (dyed orange). Inches of thread used: 6,092 cm. Number of matchsticks used: 8,600. Paints used: semigloss enamel

(International Orange) and matte enamel (Battleship Gray).

I might also mention that he is dead wrong when he says that writing and bridge building are the same thing. They are actually quite different. I know, because I am quite good at both of them.

15

GEORGE FULLER

The bridge deck is where most of the matchsticks go. Each 2.125-inch segment of the deck requires fifty-two matchsticks, which have to be glued together in a double layer with each match staggered so that the segments dovetail together and lock like LEGO blocks, end to end, plus the railing and cross members. Sixty-two of these interlocking segments make up the bridge deck, and it is important that each segment be constructed to precise tolerances.

(Am I boring you? Mr. Haughton would call this boring, but I find it quite fascinating.)

Only about a third of the matches are straight

enough to use, which is why I have already gone through sixty boxes. I am very selective and very precise. Each deck segment is glued one at a time. I made a jig out of some pieces of scrap oak so that every segment will come out exactly the same. So far I have manufactured fifty-seven of these segments, each of which has to be trimmed, sanded, painted International Orange on the side edges and bottom, and Battleship Gray on the top, or roadbed side. It is exacting work requiring tremendous concentration on the part of the bridge builder. It is much harder than writing.

I am fine-tuning the fit of two segments I glued together last night when I hear my father's booming voice from outside. At first I try to ignore it, because I do not wish to be disturbed, but the shouting goes on. I put down my Dremel tool and go upstairs.

My father is outside having a discussion with George Fuller, the man who has been staying with the Morrows. My father is wearing his canvas apron over his shirt and tie. He is wearing leather gloves and he has a pruning tool in his right hand, which tells me that he was working on the rosebushes that line the front of our house. George Fuller, dressed in khaki shorts and a yellow T-shirt, has his hairy arms crossed in front of his chest.

"What do you expect us to DO?" my father booms, gesticulating with the pruner.

"Maybe you could move your son to another bedroom."

"Another BEDROOM? How many rooms do you think we HAVE?"

"Look, Henry, I'm not trying to be the evil neighbor. I just—"

"DO YOU WANT US TO STRAP HIM TO HIS BED AND GAG HIM?"

"Henry, I just want to get a good night's sleep is all. Every other night I wake up, middle of the night, and have to listen to that yakking. Frankly, it's a little unsettling."

"DO YOU THINK IT IS NOT A PROBLEM FOR US TOO?"

"I'm sure it is, but—" His eyes find me standing in the doorway. For a second he is startled, then he slaps on this big fake smile and says, "Hey, Doug, how's it going?"

My father turns, shifting his anger from George Fuller to me. "What are you DOING?"

"Nothing," I say. "I heard some yelling."

"WE ARE NOT YELLING!"

George Fuller is edging away. "Listen, Henry, we can talk about this at another time. . . ."

My father swings his head back toward George Fuller and fixes him with his my-eyes-are-about-to-explode glare. He is squeezing his rosebush pruner so hard, his entire hand has gone dead white. George Fuller continues to edge away, back toward the Morrows'. I figure the yelling is about over now, so I back into the house and return to my bridge building.

George Fuller has been staying in the Morrow house for the past couple of years. It is a very peculiar arrangement. Andy has tried to explain it to me, but I still find it quite odd. One day George Fuller simply showed up with a U-Haul truck and moved a bunch of his furniture

into the Morrows' home and he has been staying with them ever since.

"Isn't it crowded?" I asked Andy.

Andy shrugged. "A little. But George is a nice guy, and he needed a place to live."

"It's been two years! Is he ever going to find a place of his own?"

"Keep your voice down, Dougie. You want them to move my room to the other side of the house?"

"Don't your parents want him to move out?"

"Nah. George is real handy. When's the last time you saw my dad mow the lawn? George does all the chores now. He even does my chores, on account of I'm so busy with school and football and theater and stuff."

"That makes sense," I said. And it did make sense. But I still think it's weird that this guy who isn't even a relative just moved in and sort of took over. I think it is very strange indeed. But then, my family is not so ordinary either.

16

POOPING CAT

My mother's full and proper name is Andrea Doris Louis-Hanson, but as a professional puzzle designer she is known as A. D. Louis. Ask any puzzle fanatic if they ever heard of A. D. Louis, and they will tell you she is one of the best. She can solve a crossword puzzle just as fast as she can write. And she can design one faster than most people can solve it.

A lot of modern puzzlers use computers to help them design their puzzles. Not my mother. She does it all by hand. She will sharpen an entire coffee can full of number two pencils, lay a big sheet of graph paper over the kitchen table, and go to work. My earliest memory is of sitting in my high chair eating Cheerios and watching my mother smoke cigarettes and mutter as she filled in those little squares. These days she doesn't smoke. Instead, she chews up her pencils, which can't be good for her either.

"There's some lasagna left over from last night, Douglas," she says without taking her eyes from the graph paper.

"I'm not hungry," I say.

"Then why are you perched there with your head in the freezer compartment?"

"I'm cooling it off."

Now she turns to look at me.

I say, "I think better when my head is cold."

"Douglas, that makes no sense whatsoever. The effect of temperature on the speed of thought is negligible. In any case, lower temperatures would be more likely to inhibit efficient mentation."

Did I mention that my mother has an extensive vocabulary?

I say, "It works. You should try it."

"I will do no such thing. Please close the freezer door."

I close the door as far as it will go without crushing my skull.

"Douglas, remove your head from the freezer and close the door. In the proper sequence, please."

I follow her instructions. My ears were getting cold anyway.

"What are we going to do with you?" she asks.

I understand that she isn't really looking for a response, but I give her one anyway.

"Feed me, wash my clothes, send me to college—"

"If you continue with this outré behavior, Douglas, no institution of higher learning will have you."

"They won't let me cool my head?"

"That, as you well know, is only the tip of the proverbial iceberg."

"I don't remember any icebergs in Proverbs."

"I was using the term in a general sense."

We stare at each other for a few seconds, two aliens stuck on the same asteroid.

"I'm almost done with my bridge," I say.

"That's excellent, Douglas. I'm sure it will be an extraordinary feat of engineering."

"I'm going to need some more matches."

"How many boxes do you need?"

"I think only four more."

"I'll call Mr. Pike at the hardware store."

Mr. Pike gets alarmed when a kid like me buys too many stick matches, so my mother has to call ahead to reassure him that I am not building a bomb or something.

"I should be done in about a week," I say. "You won't have to call him anymore."

She gives me a weak smile. "It is not a problem, Douglas."

"Andy's coming over for the test run."

My mother's face morphs into that frozen-faced, pop-eyed look that I call Pooping Cat. Because the Pooping Cat expression is often followed by tears or yelling, I back out of the kitchen and head downstairs to scrape the heads off some more matchsticks.

17

PRETTY GIRLS

There are six beautiful girls in school. I find it interesting that they all hang out together. Maybe they are drawn to one another by the same natural forces that make birds flock. Or maybe it is coincidence.

But the same thing is not true of guys. Andy is very handsome and charming, while I am sort of unappealing. I mean, I *could* be a good-looking guy if I wanted to. I could go back on the acne medication, and spend a bunch of money on clothes, and get my hair cut at Guzzi's, and get my teeth straightened, and take a shower every morning, and shave the few pitiful hairs off my upper lip.

If I did all those things, I would be quite handsome. But I would not be me.

I am watching the six most beautiful girls in class sitting in the lunchroom at the beautiful girls' table making birdlike beautiful girl chatter. In order of increasing beauty, they are:

Diana Spindelli
Briana Juster
Brittany Milligan
Briana Taylor
Susanne Feldman
Melissa Haverman

Some people might disagree about the exact order of beautifulness, but they would be wrong.

Today Melissa is wearing a white sweater made out of some fuzzy material. She looks like she is covered with a shirt made of snow. I try to imagine the snow melting. What do her breasts look like? I happen to know that girls' nipples come in different sizes and colors. I imagine Melissa's being of the small, pink variety. I must be imagining quite hard, because suddenly I notice that Melissa is looking right at me, and so are the five other beauties. She stands up and marches over to my table, which I happen to have all to myself.

For one insane moment I think she is going to sit down with me, but instead her lip curls in a nasty sort of way and she says in a loud voice, "WHAT are YOU staring at?"

Have I mentioned that Melissa's teeth are perfect?

I say something like, "Huh?"

"Quit STARING at me," she says in a voice even louder than before.

Everybody in the lunchroom is looking at us now. I see Mr. Timmer, the lunchroom monitor, coming toward us.

"I don't LIKE it when people STARE at me."

"I wasn't—"

"What seems to be the problem here?" Mr. Timmer interrupts.

"Mr. Timmer, Dougie won't stop staring at me. He's staring at my chest."

"Douglas—"

"I wasn't—"

"He stares at me all the time!"

"Melissa, please return to your table. Douglas, maybe you should finish your lunch facing the other way."

"But I—"

"Please, Douglas, I do not wish to debate what you were or were not doing with your eyes. Just move around to the other side of the table, and it won't be an issue. Okay?"

"Yes, sir." I walk around the table and sit with my back to the six beauties. Now I am looking at the football players' table, a collection of oversize goons, and they are all smirking at me. I wish Andy was there. He would stop the smirking. But Andy is in the second lunch period.

I eat quickly, my ears straining to pick words out of the chirping and twittering going on behind me. Are they talking about me? Do they despise me? Do they find me disgusting? I hope so. I hope I spoil their birdlike appetites.

18

THERAPY

One thing my parents have been quite clear about is that I am not to miss any more sessions with Dr. Ahlstrom. I can understand their position, as they have to pay her for the meetings I miss. Of course they could save a lot of money by not sending me at all, but they just can't seem to comprehend the logic of that.

Dr. Eleanor Ahlstrom is an aging female with a ragged, cigarette voice. I know she smokes, because I can smell it on her. Her office is in the Fairview Medical Center. Our meetings always start out exactly the same way. I walk into her consultation room. She is sitting in her complicated-looking chair with a manila folder spread across her lap, reading. After about six seconds she closes the folder, looks up, and smiles. Her teeth are blindingly white. I do not think they are real.

"Good afternoon, Douglas."

"Hi."

"Would you care to sit down?"

I sit. She looks me over. Looking for what, I do not know.

"And how are you today?" she always asks.

"I'm fine," I always say.

"And how are things at home?" she asks for the thirtieth time.

"Fine," I say, again and again.

All of this at $95 per hour, or $1.58 per minute.

"Have you been taking your medication?"

"Yes," I say. But it's not true. This is why I do not like visiting Dr. Ahlstrom. Every week I have to lie. I *hate* telling lies, even necessary ones.

"I understand your bridge is nearly completed. Remarkable!"

Apparently, she has been in contact with one of my parents.

"It's not so remarkable," I say.

"Really? A replica of the Golden Gate Bridge? It sounds quite ambitious."

I shrug. In fact, I think my bridge is beyond remarkable. It should win a prize—except that there are no prizes for model bridges.

"I plan to finish it by November seventeenth. You should come and see it sometime."

"I'd like that."

"Me and—" I catch myself just in time.

She leans forward like a cat about to pounce. "You and . . . ?"

"Nothing." I have made a pact with myself never to mention Andy in this office ever again. Dr. Ahlstrom has a weird aversion to Andy. She thinks that he is the source of all my problems. According to her, Andy's accomplishments undermine my own sense of self-esteem, or something like that. Also, every time I get in trouble, Andy is somehow involved. That might be true, but it is only a coincidence. Actually, Andy and I keep each other out of more trouble than we get each other into. But there is no explaining that to Dr. Ahlstrom.

"You and . . . ?" she says again, costing my parents another 65 cents.

"Me and . . . my parents are going to . . . Disney World." I'm lying again.

"Oh? That sounds like fun."

"Actually I'm not sure we're going. But I'd like to." That's only half a lie.

"I see."

We stare at each other for about $1.40.

"And how are things going at school?"

"Okay. Except my art teacher is mad at me for drawing the same thing all the time."

"Really? What have you been drawing?"

"I can show you."

She gets me a piece of paper and a pencil and, at $95 an hour, she watches as I sketch my latest version of the sigil. Believe it or not, I've actually been taking Mrs.

Felko's advice and trying to "loosen up" a little. My new sigil is quite arty, don't you think?

Dr. Ahlstrom examines my effort, frowning in a puzzled sort of way.

"Very interesting, Douglas. Would you like to tell me about it?"

Fat chance. I say, "It's just an interesting shape."

"What does it represent?"

"Nothing." *Liar!*

"Really? It looks like flames."

"I don't know what it is. I copied it out of a magazine." Lie number four.

She takes the paper from me. "May I keep this?"

"Sure."

She slides the paper into her manila folder.

I wonder what else she has in there.

19

END RUN

You are probably wondering about the pills.

I am supposed to take one pill every night before I go to bed. They are small, greenish blue, and triangle shaped, and if you chew them (which you are not supposed to do), they taste like bitter vanilla. The name of the drug is Proloftin.

A couple of years ago, shortly after the incident at the Tuttle place (which I still do not want to talk about), Dr. Ahlstrom prescribed the Proloftin for my anxiety. I was going through a hard time back then. My parents were keeping me in the house as punishment for the Tuttle thing. They would not let me see Andy at all. Then

Andy's parents took him on a long vacation, and I became extremely bored. In fact, it was boredom that got me started on the bridge. I had nothing else to do, so I started gluing matchsticks together. At first I used the partially burnt wooden matches that my mother used to light candles. My mother is quite fond of candles. But eventually I had to start scraping the heads off of fresh matches.

The pills helped for a while, mostly by making me sleepy. I was sleeping fourteen hours a day. Even when I was awake, I was sleepy. But they helped me cope with being locked up at home and not being able to see Andy. I didn't mind taking them. Eventually the Morrows returned from their vacation, and school started again, and my parents let me go out on my own, and I didn't see any reason to keep popping those little blue-green pills.

So I stopped taking them. The next morning, everything changed. I got As on every test at school, I stayed awake eighteen hours a day, and I got serious about building that bridge. The pills had been holding me back. I remember sitting in my window telling this to Andy.

"It's like the air cleared up," I told Andy. "School is easier, and my bridge is going great, and now I'm not sleepy all the time."

"Do your parents know you quit taking them?"

"No."

"They'll find out."

"Not if I don't tell them."

Anyway, I feel bad that my parents have to pay for pills I don't take and for therapy I don't need. But there is no way I am going back into sleepyland. For one thing, if I were taking the pills, I would never be awake enough for my late night missions to Woodland Trails.

Melissa Haverman's room is completely dark when I arrive at my post. It is 10:17. It is possible she went to bed early, or she could be watching TV, or she might not be home. Some nights she will stay out as late as 11:30. I turn up the collar of my jacket and settle into the crotch of the old oak and begin my wait. I can be very patient.

I wonder what happened to her night-light. She usually has her night-light on, even when she is asleep. Maybe it burned out.

I think about her face in the lunchroom, yelling at me, little droplets of spit flying from her mouth. What would it be like to touch those pink lips?

I wonder what she does every night after she closes her blinds.

I imagine myself crouching on the deck outside her room. How hard would it be to climb up there? Would I be able to see past the blinds?

Suddenly the branches are starkly lit by a bright yellow light from below.

A man's voice shouts, *"All right, you sick pervert, come on down!"*

I turn my face away from the light and duck behind a thick branch.

"Climb on down now!"

I climb, keeping the big branches between me and the light. My heart is pounding so hard, I can't breathe.

"There's no place for you to go!"

He's wrong about that. I scramble along a branch quick as a squirrel, away from the light. I hear the crunch of big feet on leaves. There's only one guy. I think it's Melissa's father. He's lost me for the moment—it's a big tree, and it still has most of its leaves.

"I'm not fooling around here!"

The branch I'm on is only about fifteen feet above the ground. He is circling the tree, raking the branches with the beam of light. Any second now the light will find me again.

Now or never. I let go of the branch and drop. I land on my feet and roll, leaves flying, then scramble to my feet and take off running. I hear shouts. Flashes of light hit the trees on either side of me. I run full speed through the greenway, zigzagging through the trees the way Andy weaves his way through a football field full of opponents. I am over the wall and out of Woodland Trails within a minute, but I don't slow down. I keep on running until I get home.

As I climb through the window, gasping for breath, I hear Andy's voice behind me.

"I told you you'd get caught, Dougie."

20

OUTRAGEOUS LIES

I am in my pajamas in bed with my eyes closed when the doorbell rings.

"I am asleep," I whisper, lying to myself now. "I've been in bed for an hour."

I hear my father's slippered feet stomping angrily from his bedroom to the front door, then voices. At first I can't hear what they are saying, then my father's voice cuts through the walls.

"I am *telling* you, he is *asleep in bed*. He does NOT go OUT at NIGHT!"

I hear the mutter of other voices, then my father's again:

"THIS IS OUTRAGEOUS! ARE YOU CALLING ME A LIAR?"

More muttering, then:

"OKAY! OKAY, YOU WANT TO TALK TO HIM, FINE! I'LL GO GET HIM."

Slippered, stomping footsteps approaching. The door opens.

"DOUGLAS!"

I sit up. "What? What?"

"I want you to come out here."

"I'm sleeping."

"No you're not. You are awake. Your eyes are open. Now come out here. Some men wish to speak with you."

Feigning grogginess, I crawl out of bed and shuffle down the hall after my stomping father.

A large policeman with a mustache is standing in the entryway. I do not like policemen. My heart was pounding hard before; now it's bouncing off my ribs.

"Come along, Douglas," my father says.

I edge closer. A smaller man, balding and wearing a green sweater, is standing beside the policeman. Melissa's father. They are both looking at me.

"That's him," says Mr. Haverman.

The policeman holds up his hand, silently asking Mr. Haverman to shut up. He says to me, "Well, son?" He has a nice voice.

"Well what?"

"I understand you were visiting Woodland Trails this evening."

I shake my head.

"See?" says my father. "He was in BED. I TOLD you."

A new voice enters the conversation. "What is going on here?" It's my mother, clutching the front of her bathrobe.

"Go back to BED, Andrea!" my father snaps.

She shudders as if his words were stones, then turns and shuffles back to her room.

The policeman says, "What time did you go to bed, son?"

"Nine fifty-six."

"You know the exact time?"

"I always check the clock."

"You're sure you weren't over in Woodland Trails?"

"I've been in bed," I say. "I don't even know what you're talking about."

"You're a lying little pervert," says Mr. Haverman. *"I know it was you in that tree!"*

"IF HE SAYS HE WAS SLEEPING, HE WAS SLEEPING!"

"Please, sirs," the policeman says, giving both of them a look. He steps toward me and puts his hands on my shoulders. Each hand weighs about ten pounds. "Look me in the eye, son, and tell me where you were tonight."

"I was asleep," I say, the lie coming easily. "I was sleeping in my bed."

The policeman keeps his hands on my shoulders for a few seconds as he stares into my eyes, then he turns to Mr. Haverman and says, "Sir, the boy says he's been at home."

"I *know* what he *says*. He's lying."

"I'm not lying," I lie.

"MY son is NOT A LIAR!"

"He's been harassing my daughter at school. Staring at her. Everybody knows about him."

"Sir, did you actually see him? I know you saw someone up in that tree, but did you see him clearly enough to identify him?"

"It was him."

"You might be asked to swear to that in court, sir."

Mr. Haverman's face changes. "I know it was him," he says.

The policeman releases his grip on my shoulders.

"Yes, but did you actually get a good look at his face?"

Mr. Haverman looks about to shatter.

"Would you excuse us for a moment," the policeman says to my father. He guides Mr. Haverman out the door. They stand on the front steps talking in low voices for almost two minutes, then the policeman turns to my father and says, "Sorry to have bothered you, sir. Have a good night."

My father closes the door, then stands looking at me, his face twitching and pulsing. I think he is about to start shouting again, but after several seconds of that he shakes his head wearily and says, "Go to bed, Douglas."

21

MEATBALLS

My parents think I'm socially backward because I don't have a lot of friends. I don't see it as a problem. Most kids are stupid. If I have a problem, it's that I don't like to talk about nothing. When I listen to other kids talking to each other, they mostly don't actually *say* anything.

For example, I am at my locker. Two girls are standing a few feet away. Here is what they say:

GIRL 1: So I was like, no way! But my mom, you know, she was like gonna have a fit or something.

GIRL 2: Yeah, and then, my mom, like . . . waita-
minute . . . what *is* that anyways? Can I have
one? What are they?

GIRL 1: Tangerine Sours. Have you heard about
Angela?

GIRL 2: Omigod, yes, she's got this *thing* on her foot,
y'know? It is *so* disgusting. You know?

GIRL 1: And that sweater she's wearing, can you
believe it?

GIRL 2: She's like this homeless person. Can I have
another one?

I have tried to talk like that, but it doesn't work for
me. Here is what would happen if I joined the conversation:

GIRL 1: So I was like, no way! But my mom, you
know, she was like gonna have a fit or
something.

ME: Does she have epilepsy?

GIRL 1: No, stupid!

GIRL 2: Yeah, and then, my mom, like . . . waita-
minute . . . what *is* that anyways? Can I have
one? What are they?

GIRL 1: Tangerine Sours.

ME: They put acid in the sugar to make it sour.

GIRL 2: That is so rude!

GIRL 1: Have you heard about Angela?

GIRL 2: Omigod, yes, she's got this *thing* on her foot,
y'know? It is *so* disgusting. You know?

ME: She must have plantar warts. I had plantar warts

last year. The doctor had to burn them off. It smelled weird.

GIRL 1: You are so disgusting. Get lost, worm.

I'm just not very good at small talk.

I don't see Melissa Haverman in the lunchroom, which is just as well. I have a feeling she would not be happy to see me. I carry my tray to my usual table. Today's lunch is spaghetti and meatballs, my favorite. As long as lunch is good, I don't care that no one sits with me.

I am on my thirteenth bite when something warm and wet slaps me across the forehead. Meatball chunks slide down my face on a river of red sauce. I see Freddie Perdue, one of the football goons, holding his spoon like a catapult and grinning at me. The rest of the goons are laughing.

He says, "Oops."

I wipe my face clean.

"You need another napkin, perv?" says Chuckles Gorman.

Freddie is loading another meatball onto his spoon. "Hey, peeper, get a load of this!"

He lets fly. I duck and the meatball goes sailing over my head. I hear an outraged screech from the beautiful girls' table. An instant later a plate goes flying past my ear and hits Freddie in the chest, decorating him with spaghetti squiggles on a field of red—what Mrs. Felko would call abstract expressionism.

"Food fight!" yells one of the football goons.

I hit the deck.

Meatballs

As the lunchroom erupts in a storm of meatballs, spaghetti, and screams, I am crawling wormlike for the door. I've got enough problems in my life. I don't need to be blamed for this one too.

The thing I don't understand is, tomorrow all those kids who were throwing food at one another will still be friends. They'll be laughing and making small talk and everything will be okay. But they won't be laughing and making small talk with me.

I don't understand. I think there is something wrong with them.

22

KICKS

I am running down the hall, looking for Andy to tell him about the food fight, when Mr. Dunphey, who teaches American literature, grabs me by the arm.

"Whoa, slow down, son. What's your hurry?"

"I got hit by a meatball," I say.

He takes in my sauce-coated face, and his own face turns pink. He is pressing his lips together and shaking. I think at first that he is angry, but then I realize that he is trying not to laugh. He takes a few seconds to get himself under control, then asks me who meatballed me.

"Everybody."

"Everybody?"

"There's a food fight in the cafeteria. I'm lucky they missed me with the spaghetti."

This time he can't stop himself from laughing. He lets go of my arm and walks off, shaking his head and giggling. I think maybe Mr. Dunphey has a mental disorder.

I hole up in one of the study halls and work on my sigil for the rest of the lunch period. The new version is quite exciting. It looks like a devil's face, or two people burning.

What I really like is that I am the only one who can find the letters in it. That is, until I show it to Andy, then he'll be able to read it too.

For the next couple of classes everybody is talking about the food fight. The teachers, of course, are angry. And the janitors are furious. Six kids got suspended for three days, and they have to come in after school to clean the cafeteria. One of the suspended kids was Freddie Perdue. That is what you call justice. The bad news is that there will be no ice cream or soft drink sales in the cafeteria until after the first of the year, more than seven weeks away. A lot of kids will be drinking milk or water.

I wash my face three times, but I still smell like a meatball when school lets out. Maybe I will take a shower as soon as I get home. Or maybe I'll work on my bridge for a while first.

I am walking down Fourteenth Street, thinking about the bridge, when I hear running footsteps behind me. I step to the right side, giving them room to pass, when something smacks me hard on the back of my head. I pitch forward and hit the sidewalk with my palms. My backpack goes flying, books skidding down the sidewalk.

"Where ya think yer goin', *perv*?" Freddie Perdue's voice. His size fourteen Nikes are a few inches in front of my face. I push myself up to my hands and knees; my palms are on fire and the back of my head is throbbing.

"I asked you a question, *perv*."

I look up. Freddie is not alone. He is with Ty Bridger and Aron Metz, two of his football goon friends.

"I'm going home," I say.

"You sure you aren't going over to Woodland? Gonna do some more window peeping?"

"No," I say. "That wasn't me."

"*Liar!*" Freddie draws back one enormous foot and kicks me hard in the ribs, I curl up and try to roll away, but they are on me, three of them, kicking at me from every side.

"Asshole." A boot slams into my back.

"Pervert." A tennis shoe smashes into my ear and I hear myself scream.

"Goddamn peeper." One of them stomps on my chest; air hisses from my lungs. I shape my mouth to call for Andy, but there is nothing there, no air to shout with, and then a shoe crashes into my temple, and they kick me again, and again, and I go to a place where there are no people and there is no pain, only the distant sound of rubber toes thudding into flesh and bone.

23

ROOM 317

I remember every blow. I can count them. I have made a list:

1. Hit on back of head (Freddie)
2. Kick to ribs (Freddie)
3. Kick to left leg (Aron or Ty)
4. Kick to ribs (Freddie)
5. Kick to left buttock (Aron or Ty)
6. Kick to ear (Freddie)
7. Stomp to chest (Aron)
8. Kick to right knee (Ty)
9. Kick to back (Aron or Ty)
10. Kick to ribs (Freddie)

11. Kick to back (Aron or Ty)
12. Kick to thigh (Aron or Ty)
13. Kick to temple (Freddie)

The policeman who comes to see me in the hospital in room 317 is the same policeman who came to my house. I find this to be very significant. I give him a complete report of the incident, including the list above. He was very impressed.

"You remember all that?" he says.

"I have a very organized mind."

The policeman attaches the list to his clipboard.

"Are you going to arrest them?"

He ignores my question. "Do you know why you were attacked?"

"No."

"Did it have anything to do with the food fight at school?"

"I don't know."

"You have no idea why they beat you up?"

"I think they were trying to kill me. You should arrest them for attempted murder."

"We'll see about that."

"I might have a concussion. I could have internal bleeding."

"The doctor told me you were going to be fine, son."

"I have stitches in my ear."

"They're just keeping you here overnight as a precaution. The doctor told me you'll be going home first thing tomorrow morning." The policeman stands up.

"Believe me, son, we are taking this assault very seriously."

"I have bruised ribs."

"Don't worry, son. Nobody is getting away with anything. I'll talk to these three young men. And I'll get that window peeper, too." He smiles, winks, and walks out of the room.

My mom stays with me the rest of the afternoon and evening, sitting by the side of my bed. She works on a new crossword puzzle while I lie there thinking of ways to get back at Freddie and his goons. One way would be to catch that rat that lives in the football stadium and put it in a steel box with a hole in it and strap it to Freddie with the hole against his body so that the only way for the rat to get out is to chew its way through Freddie's stomach. Or I could soak his Nikes in gasoline and light them on fire while they are on his feet. Or I could just ask Andy to beat the crap out of him.

Where is Andy, anyway? I figured he would come as soon as he heard I was in the hospital.

Of course, since Freddie will be in jail, I probably won't get a chance to do any of that, but thinking about it helps me forget about the pain in my chest, my head, and my ear.

When visiting hours are over, Andy still hasn't shown up. My mother packs up her pencils and graph paper.

"Did you tell Andy I'm here?" I ask.

She sighs. "No, dear, I did not."

"Why not?"

"I'm sorry, Douglas." She smiles her weariest smile. "I must have forgotten."

I don't sleep well in strange places, and the hospital is as strange as it gets, with all the weird noises and smells and the scratchy sheets, and it doesn't help that I still ache all over my body. I am still not asleep at 10:30 when Andy strolls into the room.

"I hear you got yourself a job as a punching bag for the football team," he says.

"How'd you get in? Visiting hours are over."

"I just walked in. Nobody said anything. I couldn't come earlier because we had rehearsals for the new play."

"That's okay."

Andy sits down next to the bed and looks closely at my torn ear. "Dougie, you're a mess!"

"It was Freddie and Ty and Aron."

"I heard. The cops picked up all three of them."

That news—and Andy's presence—make me feel much better. "They say I can go home in the morning."

Andy reaches out and rests his warm hand on my arm. "I'm glad you're okay," he says. "But I have to tell you something: I told you so."

"Told me what?"

"That you'd get in trouble for sneaking around Woodland Trails."

"Oh."

"You could have been hurt worse."

"I know. I tried to yell for you, but they stomped the air out of my chest."

"I'm sorry. I can't always be around to help you."

"I thought I was going to die."

"I won't let you die."

"I won't let you die either."

"I know." I see the tears gathering in his blue eyes, and tides of joy wash over me. He cares. He really cares what happens to me. And he is the only one who understands.

24

NUMBER FIVE

My parents keep me home from school for the rest of the week. That's fine with me. I spend the time working on my bridge. My ribs hurt, my palms are scraped and sore, my stitched-up ear itches, and I have a headache that won't go away—but it hurts just as much to do nothing at all. I've completed the towers, the anchors, and all the bridge deck segments. I've strung the main cables. I've dyed the thread I'm using for the suspender cables, or stringers. Now I'm hanging the bridge deck from the 162 pairs of vertical stringers. Each pair of stringers takes about fifteen minutes. On the actual Golden Gate Bridge the stringers had to be adjusted to a fraction of an inch. On my bridge, the leeway is hundredths of an inch. The work is intricate and precise.

Late Thursday afternoon I am installing stringer pair number thirty-seven when the doorbell rings. I hear my mother, then another woman's voice, then double footsteps. I hear my mother saying, "I'm so sorry! With Douglas injured, and everything else going on, we simply forgot to call you."

"That's quite all right." I recognize the voice now. It's Dr. Ahlstrom. "I've been meaning to drop by in any case. Douglas has been talking so much about the little bridge he's working on."

"Little?" My mother laughs. They are at the top of the stairs now, and she calls down, "Douglas, you have company, dear."

I don't say anything right away. I hate being interrupted when I am doing precision work.

"Douglas?"

"I hear you."

"May we come down?"

"Okay. I guess."

I watch their feet coming down the basement steps, one through thirteen, and then I see my mother's face and then I see Dr. Ahlstrom's face.

"Good afternoon, Douglas," she says. And then she sees the bridge and her chin drops and she says, "Good Lord. Douglas. Oh my God."

"I told you," I said.

"Douglas, I had no idea." Dr. Ahlstrom is only the fifth living person ever to see my bridge. Me, Andy, and my parents are the four others.

"It's . . . it's beautiful," Dr. Ahlstrom says, and I feel my blood bubbling with oxygen.

"It's not done yet," I say.

"Yes, but, my goodness, Douglas." She approaches the bridge and looks at the details, at each carefully shaped and fitted matchstick, at the perfect joints and precise alignment of the parts. For a moment I see it through her eyes. It seems impossible that anything made by hand could be so precise and flawless.

She reaches out a hand to touch it.

"Don't!" I slap her hand back.

"Douglas!" my mother says.

Dr. Ahlstrom clutches her slapped hand and looks at me with wide eyes.

"I'm in the middle of hanging the suspender cables," I say. "Nothing can move."

"It's all right," says Dr. Ahlstrom. She gives me her professional smile. "It's a remarkable model, Douglas. What inspired you to build it?"

"Bridges are important. They connect things. You need them to get from one side to the other."

"That's very interesting."

That's what she says when she's trying to get me to talk. I am not in the mood.

I say, "Are you going to charge my parents for coming here today?"

"Douglas!" my mother says, horrified. Anything to do with money embarrasses my parents. I don't know why.

"It's all right," Dr. Ahlstrom says to my mother. "Douglas and I are often quite honest and direct with each other." She turns back to me. "As you know, I bill 50 percent of my consultation fee for missed appointments, Douglas. I'm not charging any additional fee for my visit here, as it was something I decided to do on my own."

"Okay then," I say.

Nobody says anything for three or four seconds.

"I have to get back to work," I say.

25

RESCHEDULED

When I go back to school on Monday, everything is different. As soon as I walk in the door I can feel it. Everybody is looking at me. People who never knew I was alive before are staring at me like I'm a freak. I pretend not to notice. I go straight to my locker and drop off my backpack. People slow down as they walk past, staring at the stitches in my ear. I ignore them.

When I get to calculus, before I sit down at my desk, Mr. Kesselbaum tells me to report to Principal Janssen. Everyone (including Melissa Haverman) watches me walk out of the classroom. The kid who got beat up. The kid with stitches in his ear.

In the front office I sit on the bench and wait until the secretary calls me into the principal's office. Inside, Principal Janssen and Ms. Neidermeyer, the school counselor, are waiting for me, wearing two of the phoniest smiles I've ever seen.

"Good morning, Douglas. We're glad to see you up and around again," says Principal Janssen. Janssen is big, fat, small featured, and soft voiced. He always wears corduroys, colorful sweaters, and slip-on shoes. His eyes are the color of mud.

Ms. Neidermeyer is the exact opposite of Principal Janssen: skinny, shrill, wide mouthed, big nosed, sharp chinned, red nailed, and wearing a crisp navy blue outfit.

"How are you?" she asks. They are the first three words she has ever spoken to me. Why is she acting like we're old friends?

"Have a seat," says Principal Janssen.

I sit in one of the plastic chairs in front of his desk.

"I guess you had a pretty rough week," he says.

"I got beat up," I say.

"Yes, and you had that little run-in with the police."

I shrug. "They thought I was somebody else."

Nobody speaks for what seems like five minutes, but it was probably only a few seconds.

Principal Janssen clears his throat. "Yes, well, I know you've been having some problems with some of the other students. . . ."

"I don't have a problem. I just want to be left alone."

"Yes, well, ah . . . we've made some, ah, adjustments in your class schedule. . . ." He looks at Ms. Neidermeyer.

"We thought it best to change your lunch period,

Douglas. We don't want another incident like last Tuesday."

"Incident?"

"The food fight."

"That wasn't me."

"Nevertheless, don't you think it would be best for you to eat your lunch at a different time than Freddie Perdue and his friends?"

"What difference does that make? They're in jail, aren't they?"

Uncomfortable silence ensues.

Principal Janssen shifts in his chair. "Well . . . no," he says.

"How can they not be in jail?"

"I know you're upset about what happened—"

"They tried to kill me!"

"Douglas, please sit down. . . . Thank you."

I am shaking.

"Douglas, we want you to know we believe you. Those kids were up to no good. The police brought them in and talked to them. All three of them denied harming you. I'm afraid it's a case of your word against theirs."

"Theirs is wrong."

Ms. Neidermeyer reaches out a red-nailed hand and touches my arm. "We know that, Douglas."

I shrug away her touch. "It's not fair."

"No, it's not. But we're trying to make the best of the situation. We've designed a new schedule for you. You'll be moving to the second lunch period and changing from Mrs. Felko's afternoon art class to the morning class, and you'll be in Study Hall C after your lunch period."

"Why do *I* have to change? Why don't you change *their* schedules?"

Principal Janssen says, "It simply was not practical, Douglas."

I hug myself to stop the shaking. It doesn't help.

"They should all be in jail," I say. "You should at least kick them out of school. You're responsible for my safety."

"Douglas, we have a responsibility to be fair to *all* of our students. I don't know exactly what happened between you and those three boys, but I'm sure that their attack was not completely unprovoked. Things like that don't just happen. I don't know what you did to anger Freddie Perdue, and frankly I don't want to know, but you must realize that you had a part in it."

I gape at him, hardly able to believe what he is saying.

Ms. Neidermeyer says, "No one is saying you deserved to be injured, Douglas. We're just trying to make the best of a very unfortunate situation."

"I've spoken with Freddie and Aron and Ty," says Principal Janssen. "They know that if they bother you—if one of them so much as touches you—they'll be expelled. I promise you won't have any problem with them."

I feel sick.

"Oh, and one more thing. We've moved you to the last period calculus class. Your first period class will now be language arts."

"Why did you do that?"

"We thought it would be best for you."

For a moment I am more confused than ever. Then I realize that first period calculus is the only class I share with Melissa Haverman.

They are trying to keep me away from Melissa.

26

FLAMMABLE

The one good thing about my new schedule is that Andy and I have lunch at the same time. We grab one of the empty tables in back and I tell him about my meeting with Principal Janssen and Ms. Neidermeyer. The more I talk about it, the madder I get.

"I don't see why they're messing around with my schedule when I didn't do anything wrong."

"Well, you *did* get caught window peeping."

"I didn't get *caught*."

"I mean, none of this would have happened if you hadn't gone to Woodland Trails."

"You're as bad as the rest of them. No, you're worse. You're supposed to be my friend."

"I *am* your friend, Dougie."

"Then you should go beat the crap out of Freddie Perdue."

"Is that what you want?"

"I want you to beat the crap out of all of them: Freddie, Ty, Aron, Mr. Janssen, and Melissa's dad."

"Okay, I'll beat 'em up, but after they catch me, will you come visit me in prison?"

"You won't go to prison. Freddie didn't."

"Yeah, but he didn't beat up five people. Just you."

"Ha-ha. Hey, what time does this lunch period end?"

"It's almost over." He stands up and points at the clock on the wall behind me. "I gotta get to Spanish."

I turn my head to look at the clock. Two sophomores at the next table are staring at me.

"What are *you* looking at?" I ask.

"Nothing," one of them says.

"You're looking at *something*." The bell rings. "I don't like being stared at," I say.

"Sorry." The sophomores pick up their trays and head for the trash.

I turn back to Andy, but he is gone.

According to my new schedule I am supposed to go to Study Hall C, but the idea of sitting in a crowded study hall with a bunch of kids staring at me makes my stomach hurt. I can hardly endure being inside this building. I think of Principal Janssen and a clot of anger, a burning sensation, forms high in my chest. My bruised ribs throb and my teeth grind against each other and I imagine him one inch tall and me driving over him with the Madham Special.

Dr. Ahlstrom says I should be careful when I get angry. She says that anger is powerful and difficult to control and that when I feel myself boiling over I should take a walk. I look out the glass doors of the south exit. Outside it is bright and sunny, a beautiful November day, almost seventy degrees. I walk out of the school. I have no destination, but my feet seem to know where I'm going. As I walk I feel my anger growing. I'm mad at Freddie and his bunch, sure, but I'm even madder at Principal Janssen and Ms. Neidermeyer. And the cops. And Melissa's father. I'm mad at all the kids who stared at me and all the kids who didn't. And I'm mad at Andy. I let my anger twist and turn. I imagine terrible fates for each one of my tormentors, my betrayers, my persecutors. When I reach the chain-link fence surrounding the football stadium, I turn back to look at the school. The red brick walls look heavy and cold and indestructible.

I follow the fence around to the gate. It is open. I enter the stadium and climb to the top tier of seats and sit in the sun and open my notebook. I begin to draw the sigil, tracing the invisible curves and lines in my head. The sigil mutates. The letters are almost impossible to see now, but I know they are there, tangled within the fire, fighting to escape.

I stare at the completed sigil and feel my anger drain into it.

As I stare into its twists and curves I imagine licks of flame and searing heat. I look over at the school and imagine the bricks and steel melting into slag.

And I see someone walking toward me.

It's Andy.

"Hey," he says, sitting down next to me. "Watching the game?"

"I'm processing my anger," I say.

"Is that like processing cheese?" He grins.

A few minutes ago I was mad at him, but now I see his smile and listen to his incredibly stupid joke and all my anger melts away. How could I stay mad at Andy?

"Yeah, it's like cheese," I say.

"What are you drawing? Is that a fire?"

"It's a flaming sigil."

"Oh, cool!"

"So how come *you're* here? I thought you had Spanish class."

"I looked out the window and I saw you sitting out here, so I told Mrs. Garcia I had to go throw up." He laughs. "You know what she said? She said, 'You don't look so sick to me, but okay, you go *vómito.*'"

"What if she looks out the window and sees you?"

"She won't. So, I guess you're pretty mad at everybody."

"You could say that. I'm thinking about burning down the school. Only I don't think brick is flammable."

"You're quite mad, you know," he says in a British accent, doing James Bond.

"Not mad, disturbed."

"Okay, disturbed. But let's not burn down the school. I've got a better idea."

"What's that?"

"You got any change?"

I dig in my pocket and come out with a quarter and three dimes.

Andy stands up. "C'mon."

27

POWER

This is power: You drop a metal disk into a slot in a metal box, speak a few carefully chosen words into a black plastic contrivance, and minutes later seventeen hundred people (give or take a few) instantly drop whatever they are doing and file out of a huge red brick building into the sunlight.

Andy and I watch from across the street, then slip into the throng. Several teachers are trying to herd us toward the stadium. Everybody is talking and moving and bouncing off each other, tossing misinformation back and forth:

"...just a drill ..."

". . . fire in the basement . . ."

I get separated from Andy in the confusion of bod-ies and am absorbed into the crowd.

". . . somebody got shot."

"Omigod, who got shot?" says a dark-haired girl to my right.

"It's a bomb threat," I say, getting into the spirit of it, enjoying being part of the crowd, bumping against her with my shoulder.

She gives me a nasty look and moves away, but I hear her tell someone there's a bomb in the school.

". . . gonna blow up the school . . ."

". . . probably a gas leak . . ."

". . . I feel sick . . ."

I am craning my neck, looking for Andy, when I see Melissa Haverman. I move toward her, but she sees me coming and her eyes go wide and she moves away. I'm cut off by a tight clot of sophomores.

"I heard there's a bomb," I say, trying to break through.

They don't hear me. There are too many voices.

". . . fire in the chemistry lab . . ."

". . . practice drill . . ."

". . . terrorists . . ."

". . . I heard it was gas . . ."

". . . poison gas . . ."

". . . explosion . . ."

". . . killed . . ."

The shouts of the teachers are lost in the shuffling and chatter, and I lose track of Melissa. Two police cars show up just as the last people leave the building. They get out their bullhorns and help herd us to the stadium. We squeeze in four abreast through the gates and spill onto the field. Kids are looking for their friends, trying to gather into their cliques and clubs and friends and subcultures—jocks looking for jocks, boyfriends seeking girlfriends, pretty girls looking for the other pretty girls, goth seeking goth—but we are being herded mercilessly, the cops and the teachers teaming up to organize the mass of students. It takes about twenty minutes to get us all into the stands and seated. I can't see Andy anywhere.

I am sitting between two guys I don't know and who don't know me.

One of them says, "This is so stupid."

"How do you know?" I ask him.

"It's just some sort of prank. Somebody pulled the fire alarm or something."

"It's not a fire alarm," I tell him. "It's a bomb threat."

"How do you know?"

"I heard one of the teachers say so. I think it's serious."

"Seriously stupid, maybe. When's the last time you heard of a school blowing up?"

"That doesn't mean it couldn't be real."

"It's just some jerkball with a phone. It's *always* some idiot with a phone."

"You don't know what you're talking about," I say, a bit nettled. "You don't know who it was, and you don't know if there's a bomb."

"You'll see," he says.

One of the teachers—no, it's Principal Janssen—has borrowed a bullhorn from one of the cops.

"ATTENTION . . . could I have your attention,

please!" He gives the chatter a few seconds to die down. "As you all probably know by now, we received a phone call from someone claiming to have planted a bomb in the school—"

"I told you," I say to the kid on my right. He ignores me.

"In all likelihood," Principal Janssen continues, "this is a misguided prank. The police are going through the building right now. The process will take them about two hours, which will take us to the end of the school day—"

A weak cheer emanates from parts of the stands and several students stand up as if to leave.

"Sit DOWN. This is NOT cause for celebration, and NO ONE is leaving until two fifty. This is a serious matter. It is serious any time there is a threat to our safety. And I promise you, we will find the person or persons behind this, whether or not that threat is real, and they will be held accountable."

He goes on for a while but eventually winds down. Conversation in the stands is mostly speculation about who might have phoned in the bomb threat. The most popular theory is that it was a student from St. Andrew Valley High, our rival school. A couple of the goth kids are also mentioned, just because they wear black and act spooky.

I don't hear anyone mention me or Andy.

28

TRAINS AND LOCKERS

News of the bomb threat does not make anything easier at home. My mother sees it as another excuse to put me in a private school. My father, naturally, is opposed. He uses logic to make his point:

"DO YOU KNOW HOW MUCH THOSE PLACES COST?"

"Yes, but his school is receiving bomb threats. How can he learn properly in such an environment?"

"THERE WAS NO BOMB!"

My mother starts shaking, but she doesn't give up.

"The Catholic school isn't that expensive—"

"WE AREN'T CATHOLIC!"

"You don't have to be Catholic, and they have a very good program—"

"WHAT DID I JUST SAY?"

And so on. Of course, my father has logic on his side, and he can yell louder, so I'm pretty sure I'm not going to Catholic school anytime soon.

That night I dream of fires and explosions and student bodies moving in great masses from one building to another and bumping into Melissa Haverman. I bump her again and again, but she won't look at me. And then Andy is there, floating like a ghost, laughing at me. I wake up. The room is dark. My clock reads 3:17, the same number as my room at the hospital. Seventeen everywhere. I am seventeen. Seventeen is the seventh prime number. I sit up in bed and listen. All is silent. I go to the window and open it. Andy's window is shut. The blinds are closed. I call out his name once, but I know he won't hear me. After a time I return to bed and close my eyes and imagine a train passing. The engine has long passed; the end of the train is nowhere in sight. I count the cars: boxcar, container car, Pressureaide freight car, tank car, tank car, tank car, Coalveyor, boxcar, boxcar, passenger car. . . .

In the morning everybody at school is talking about the bomb threat. I weave through the crowded halls, everyone ignoring me. I stop at my locker and spin the combination lock. . . .

Something is wrong. The lock feels wrong. It turns too easily, without the usual faint clicking. I pull up on the handle and the door swings open and I stare at the contents.

Someone has been in my locker.

I sort through my stuff to see what is missing. My books are there, and my extra sweatshirt, and my file folders full of old papers. . . .

Someone's hand comes down on my shoulder and I jump.

"Easy, Douglas." It's Principal Janssen.

"Someone broke into my locker," I say.

"It's okay, Douglas. We need you down at the office."

His hand is still gripping my shoulder.

"Somebody was in my locker!"

Kids are stopping in the hall, staring at us. I guess I was yelling.

"Come along," says Principal Janssen, pulling me away from the locker.

"My stuff!"

"No one will bother your stuff." He shifts his grip to my upper arm. I see flashes of faces as he moves me quickly down the hall, I try to keep up, but my feet barely touch the floor. Everyone we pass is looking at us. Looking at me.

29

INTERROGATION

Principal Janssen's office is on the east side of the building. The morning sun slices through the aluminum blinds, puncturing my skull like a bright yellow knife. Their eyes are cutting at me too. Six eyes: Janssen, Ms. Neidermeyer, and the cop. The same cop who accused me of spying on Melissa Haverman. The same mustached cop who visited me in the hospital and who refused to put my attackers in jail where they belong.

"Douglas, this is Officer John Hughes. He is with the Juvenile Affairs Division of the Fairview Police Department."

Officer Hughes gives me a small nod.

"We've met," I say.

Principal Janssen clears his throat. "We'd like to talk about yesterday afternoon, Douglas. Do you have anything to tell us?"

"What do you mean?" I say, all innocent and bewildered.

The three of them exchange glances. Ms. Neidermeyer leans forward in her chair.

"Douglas, we know who called in the bomb threat yesterday."

For the next seventeen seconds there is much staring and waiting. I finally break the silence. "Well? Are you going to tell me who it was?"

"Douglas, you know who it was. You were seen."

"Seen where?"

"Several students saw you in the football stadium just before the phone call."

"I was in the stadium," I say. "It was my study hall period. I was working on an art project. Do you want to see it?"

"No," says Principal Janssen. "What we want, young man, is for you to come clean with us. We know you called in that bomb threat."

"No I didn't," I say, looking him straight in the eye.

He seems surprised by that. Leaning forward, he ticks off several points on his fingers.

"You were seen in the stadium at one thirty. A few minutes later you left the stadium. At 1:39, the bomb threat call was made from the pay phone outside of Gunnerson's Market, one block from the stadium." He pauses, fixing his muddy eyes on me. "You made that call, Douglas."

"It wasn't me."

"Yes, Douglas, it *was* you. A cashier at Gunnerson's Market recognized you."

"You're lying," I say. I was keeping a lookout when Andy made the call. No one saw us. The cashier must be lying—or Janssen is lying about what the cashier said—because if somebody had really seen us at the phone they would have seen us both. I feel myself getting all scrambled inside, like my thoughts are getting tangled in my intestines. Are they letting Andy off the hook because he is on the football team? Or do they have him in another room? Maybe he is being interrogated right now by the vice principal, the football coach, and the chief of police. I've seen it on TV: divide and conquer. But Andy would never betray me. He wouldn't.

"We're not lying, Douglas. We're giving you a chance to own up to your actions. This is a serious matter, and I'll be straight with you—you will not be allowed to continue as a student here at Fairview Central. Our zero tolerance policy is quite clear on that."

"But I didn't DO anything!" My voice sounds weird. Am I shouting? I try to bring it back down. "How do you know it wasn't somebody from St. Andrew Valley?"

"Douglas, the question is not who made the phone call. We know it was you. The question now is whether you will be prosecuted to the full extent of the law. You are seventeen years old—you're not a little kid anymore. An offense such as this could result in jail time."

The thought of being locked in a room fills me with vacuum, a bottomless internal pit of dread sucking at my organs, threatening to devour me from within. I can't believe they would put an innocent person in jail. My parents would never let them. I look at the cop, John Hughes. I look at his mustache, at his thick nose, at his heavy-lidded eyes. He stares at me as if I'm an animal, like a dog who crapped on the kitchen floor.

"It wasn't me," I say. My voice sounds distant and weak.

I hear a bell go off. Is first period over already? Have we been sitting in this office for forty-five minutes? I look at my interrogators, like statues, silent and unblinking. The silence is heavy and hollow and unbearable; it cries out to be filled.

"It wasn't me," I hear myself say again.

For the first time, Officer Hughes speaks: "Are you sure you want to go to prison, son?"

Something—maybe it is my liver—crumbles. I am getting smaller.

"Have you ever been locked in a cell?"

I am having trouble breathing.

"Son? Don't you think it's time?"

I shake my head, but my mouth is forming words. I try to freeze my lips, but the words are already flying through the air at the speed of sound.

"It was Andy." I can't believe I'm ratting out my best friend. "Andy Morrow. Andy made the call. I was with him. I saw him. It was Andy. Oh my God." I think I must be crying now. My face is wet. Ms. Neidermeyer is leaning toward me, eyes wide, arms out to embrace me. I slap her hands away and gulp air and shout at the walls, "I'm sorry! I'm sorry, Andy!"

30

INTERROGATION (PART 2)

"I understand that you've been seeing Andy again, Douglas."

I pretend not to hear her. I really don't want to get into this. I'd much rather talk about my bridge.

"Douglas?"

"What?"

"How long has this been going on?"

You would think she would want to talk about my bridge. "How long has what been going on?" I say.

"How long have you been seeing Andy?"

The easiest thing is to tell her what she wants to hear. "I haven't," I say.

"Your mother tells me you've been talking to yourself at night."

"Maybe."

"What do you talk about?"

"We talk about the bridge."

"We?"

"Me and myself."

She makes a note in her folder.

"Have you been taking your medication?"

I don't answer her right away.

"Douglas?"

"I might have forgot a few times."

She makes another note.

"Who called the bomb threat in to the school?"

"They say it was me."

"And was it?"

"It was . . ." I remember it clearly. Andy putting the coins into the pay phone and punching in the number. Grinning at me. I can see his fingers gripping the phone and his white teeth as he speaks.

I know Dr. Ahlstrom wants me to lie now. I close my eyes. I see fire. I feel it warm on my face and hands. I sink into it.

"Douglas?"

I open my eyes. "What?"

"What were you thinking about?" She's peering at me. I am a specimen on a slide.

"Trains," I lie.

"Who called in the bomb threat, Douglas?"

"It was Andy." I slump down in the chair and wrap my arms around myself.

"Douglas, Andy is not with us anymore. You know that."

I glare at her. She is so wrong. She doesn't know how wrong she is.

"Andy Morrow died nearly three years ago, Douglas. You remember that, don't you?"

I close my eyes. The fire is hotter now.

"Douglas?"

"What?"

"Andy is dead."

I shake my head, marveling at her stupidity. I say, "You think he died at the Tuttle place, don't you?"

She nods and says softly, "That's right, Douglas. Don't you remember? It was a cold day."

I remember the cold. A cold early spring day. Andy and I were in the Tuttle house. I was carving the sigil in the floorboards with my Swiss Army knife. Lying on my belly, staring into the hard, polished floor, dragging the knife blade across the grain of the maple flooring. We had been talking for hours. The sun had fallen behind a bank of clouds.

"I'm cold," Andy said. Or maybe it was me who said it.

"We could build a fire," I said. Or maybe Andy said it. I think it was me.

Andy found a broken chair in one of the upstairs bedrooms, and there were some dusty old boards and newspapers in the basement. We broke up the chair and built a loose pile of paper and wood in the fireplace. I had a book of matches in my pocket. I lit the fire and we watched as the paper flickered and fluffed into tongues of flame, and the dry boards caught and filled the fireplace with heat and hissing and the dull, distant roar of hot air rushing up the chimney. We sat on the floor close by the fire, throwing on chunks of chair and broken pieces of board whenever the fire slackened.

"If we'd had a fireplace in the tree house, it never would've burned," I said.

"We should build another one."

"Another fire?"

"No, stupid, another tree house."

"That would be cool."

I remember the conversation, but not who said what.

"Douglas?"

"What?"

"What do you remember?"

"It was Andy."

"What was?"

"The knife."

We fell asleep in front of the fire on that hardwood floor. We drifted off, each of us to our own dreams. Then came the nightmare: a roaring, sucking monster shaking me and shouting, "Doug! Wake up!"

I claw my way out of the dream and Andy's fingers are digging into my shoulders and it is dark and orange. We are under a cloud; the room is filled with smoke. The fireplace is roaring. The bottom few feet of the room is clear, but above us is a layer of dense black smoke.

"The house is on fire," Andy shouts.

I jump to my feet. The smoke is low and thick. I take in a lungful and double over, coughing. Andy pulls me back down to the floor.

"We gotta get out of here!" We head for the front
door on our hands and knees and a few seconds later we
are outside.

The top of the house is in flames. A huge spire of
flame is coming from the chimney.

"We're in big trouble now," Andy says.

"We got out," I say.

"*You* got out, Douglas. Andy didn't."

"Yes he did." I'm shaking. "We got out of the house.
We were watching it burn. . . ."

"I forgot my Victorinox," I said to Andy.

"The one I gave you?"

"I left it by the fireplace."

Andy looks at me as if I left a part of him inside that
burning house. And suddenly he is running back toward
the front door. I shout after him, but I don't know what.
He is in the house. He is inside, and the house is burning. I imagine him bent over running through the foyer
into the living room, seeing the red plastic handle of the
Swiss Army knife, grabbing it, heading back toward the
front door. . . .

Where is he?

The house is engulfed in flame.

I shout his name. I run toward the front door, but it's
too hot, I can't get close. I can't get in.

"He went back in," I say. I'm not shaking anymore.

Dr. Ahlstrom nods. "You remember now."

"He went in to get my knife.'"

"That's very good, Douglas."

"I don't like thinking about it," I say.

"I don't blame you."

"Everybody blames me."

"That's not true."

"I blame me."

"Well, maybe we can do something about that." She is writing in her folder again. "I'm giving you a new prescription for a slightly higher dosage of Proloftin, and I don't want you to skip any doses this time, all right?"

"I still see him," I say. "He still lives next door."

Dr. Ahlstrom is shaking her head. "No he doesn't, Douglas. Andy's parents moved away a few months after he passed away. Someone else has been living in the Morrow house for the past three years, a man named Fuller."

"But I see Andy."

"Not anymore." She hands me a slip of paper. "This is your new prescription. I believe your mother is waiting for you outside. I'd like to speak with her for a moment. Perhaps you could ask her to step inside?"

I let myself out of the interrogation room. Everything looks sharp edged and bright, even my mother.

"She wants to see you," I say.

31

GODZILLA

The new pills are larger and bluer, but they are still shaped like triangles. My mother watches as I put one in my mouth and swallow it with a gulp of water. I feel it tumble slowly down my esophagus. My mother smiles, and I head downstairs to work on my bridge.

I once read a magazine article that said that Proloftin was originally derived from a powerful rhinoceros tranquilizer used by zookeepers. I believe it. One moment you are standing in a room painfully bright with sunlight, and an hour later someone has pulled the shades and you want to take a nap. But this larger dose hits me like a sledgehammer. I am fitting the last deck segment into my bridge and . . .

. . . time . . .

. . . passes . . .

I become aware of a small wooden contrivance in my hand. Interesting. It is made of matchsticks fastened together with some sort of adhesive substance, a protein or collagen of some sort. . . . What is it called? The word eludes me. I turn the assemblage in my hand. Somehow I know that it is part of a bridge.

Ah, yes, the adhesive substance is called glue. I smile happily, joyfully, ecstatically, Proloftily. The answer is glue. How nice it is to know glue.

. . . time . . .

. . . passes . . .

I am looking at a bridge constructed upon an enormous table. Somehow I know that it was I who constructed this marvelous object. My fingers, ingers, bingers, lingers. . . .

. . . time . . .

. . . passes . . .

The effects of Proloftin peak during the first hour, after which you begin to think again. Think, stink, bink, fink . . . I start laughing uncontrollably . . . and suddenly it is not funny. I want to weep. I am holding a section of bridge deck in my hand, and there is the bridge, bright orange—*International* Orange—and unearthly in its complexity. I must insert the final section into place. Lace. Ace.

But where? I am thinking, but my thoughts are sluggish and scrambled.

Wait.

I am remembering something.

Maybe not.

It doesn't matter.

I drop the deck section on the floor. The bridge is not important. What is important? I cast about blindly through the murk in my head. Names tumble through my head: Douglas. Haverman. Andy. MacArthur. Morrow. Hanson. Melissa. Mother. Freddie. Eddie. Die. I . . . I am thrown into a room filled with dangerous memories. A burning house. This should bother me, but my heart is numb. I stare without feeling as Andy runs into the burning house.

He is in there.

He is still in there.

Somewhere in my head a switch closes and I remember something that gives me a flash of hope. The knife. A few days after the fire, I remember Andy showing up at my window and giving me my knife.

"I saved it," he said with a grin.

If Andy died in the fire, how could he have returned my knife to me?

I know where it is, in one of the old cigar boxes I use to store train parts. I start opening boxes and, on the third one, I find it. But instead of seeing a bright red plastic handle and seventeen shiny tools, I find a blackened, frozen, twisted metal mess. It's the knife, but this knife has been through a holocaust. A bleak and depressing memory drudges into my head. I remember climbing through the ruins of the Tuttle place, weeks after the fire. I remember kicking through the charred remains of the house, my shoes and jeans black with soot, and then finding the blackened, melted corpse of the knife. . . .

He never came out.

Andy is dead.

Nothing is important. No thing.

I reach out my hand. My fingers curl around a section of bridge. I am King Kong, Godzilla, Galactus. I squeeze. I hear the crackle of matchsticks.

. . . pain . . .

. . . passes . . .

I am sitting on the concrete floor and I can smell the sour, tangy reek of resinous pine. The smell of matchsticks. The smell of phosphorous. The smell you get just before a fire. I sit there with the smell and a brain as thick and fibrous as a wet, wadded woolen sweater. I remember some things. I remember Andy's parents putting their house up for sale. And then George Fuller moved in.

But Andy never left. Andy died . . . but he didn't. I

know this should upset me, but I just sit there on the cold floor and let my mind go dead.

Eventually my mother's voice reaches me. It is time for dinner, that thing we do every night, that thing where you push digestible matter into your mouth hole.

I can do that. I climb to my feet.

The bridge. Something has attacked the bridge.

Interesting.

The bridge has taken serious damage to its eastern approach ramp.

I wonder whether anyone will bother to repair it.

32

THE YELLING

Morning comes gray as ash. I shuffle out of my room down the hall to the kitchen, where my mother is working on one of her crossword puzzles. She looks up from her graph paper and smiles.

"Good morning, dear."

"G'morning."

A place is set for me at the table. A greenish blue pill on a white plate on a dark green placemat on the maple table. And a glass of orange juice. And a box of cornflakes. Carton of milk. Bowl.

"Take your pill, dear, and have some breakfast."

"They make me sleepy."

"Dr. Ahlstrom said that will pass. You'll get used to it."

"They make everything fuzzy and gray."

"That's just a temporary effect, dear." She watches as I put the pill in my mouth and swallow some orange juice, then returns her attention to her puzzle. As soon as she is not looking I spit the pill into my hand and crush it and rub the wet powder into my pajama leg.

The effects of Proloftin wear off slowly. I spend most of the day in bed reading model railroading magazines. I am afraid to go into the basement. I remember hurting the bridge. I am afraid of what I might find down there.

Late in the afternoon I put my magazines aside and begin work on a new sigil. My brain is starting to work again, and guiding the felt tip pen over the lines and curves of the sigil seems to help me focus. By the time my mother calls me for dinner, I have completed it. It is an angry sigil.

"And how are you feeling this evening, Doug?" my father asks.

"Okay. I'm feeling okay. A little sleepy is all."

"Well, you need the sleep," my mother says. "You've had quite a week."

I nod.

"Dr. Ahlstrom assures us that the new dose you're on will have you back in shape in no time."

"Good." I push green leaves into my mouth and chew.

My father says, "I've taken the day off from work tomorrow."

I chew.

"I thought the three of us could take a drive."

I look up. "Where?"

"Well, as you know, you can't go back to Fairview High. We need to find a new school for you. We'd like you to take a look at St. Stephen's Academy."

I've heard of St. Stephen's Academy. It's where kids like Freddie Perdue get sent.

"Isn't that, like, some sort of prison?" I ask.

"Don't be ridiculous. It's a private school."

I stare at my father, at his craggy features and whiskers and cavernous eyes. He is a stranger. A man who comes to our house at night and shouts and mows the lawn in a suit and tie and goes to work in the morning.

"I don't think I want to go," I say.

Now he is going to start yelling, I think. But he only smiles a ghastly smile and says, "Why don't we just talk about it in the morning, Doug."

"You want to get rid of me."

"No, we don't," my mother says. "We just want to do what's best for you."

"Then forget about it. I'm not going."

My father's eyes flicker and burn. "You'll DO what we TELL you to do." The veins on his forehead start to show.

The yelling is about to begin.

33

RESTORATION

I go straight to bed after my father gets tired of yelling. I pull the covers over my face and stare into the dark. Images tumble through my brain like bedsheets and underwear in a clothes dryer: my father's red, veiny face; fire; and the people of Madham scurrying about. I see a long white hallway that frightens me. I try to think about Melissa Haverman, but her image is slippery; I can't grab hold. It must be the Proloftin. I grip the blanket and ride out the slide show.

After an hour or an eternity my mind settles, and I feel sleep rising up to engulf me. I fight it. I'm afraid that as soon as I drop off, something will come scratching at my window, and I'll be too scared to look. What if it's Andy? What if it's not?

To fend off sleep, I start counting by 17s. I lose track somewhere around 1,003—the remnants of yesterday's Proloftin are still clogging up my head. I start over. This time I get up over 2,700 before I lose track. I start to get anxious. What if the Proloftin made me as permanently moronic as Freddie Perdue? I start again, slowly, fixing each number in my mind before moving on to the next.

I am at 10,166 when I hear my parents begin their nightly ritual. I hear the water running in the bathroom sink, the sound of my mother's electric toothbrush, and their low voices, talking about whatever it is they talk about. Probably me. I wait until I hear their bedroom door close, then quietly slip out of my room and down the basement stairs.

I want to cry. Godzilla, or whatever possessed me last night, has destroyed one end of the bridge. I survey the damage. The east end of the bridge deck is broken, the suspension cables torn, the deck plates broken, the railing crushed. For a long time I simply stand, staring.

Then I get to work, salvaging what I can and rebuilding as necessary. Most of the bridge deck sections are still usable, but some of them are completely broken. I have to scrape the heads off another box of matches to build two new deck sections. As always I put the scrapings into a Mason jar. After more than 20,000 matches, I have three jars full of red phosphorus.

I get into a rhythm. My hands do the work quickly.

The last molecules of Proloftin leave my body, and my mind spins free. I think about Andy.

I am not irrational. I remember the fire. I know that Andy was inside the house when it burned. I saw his obituary. I went to his funeral. Andy died. I remember that.

But I also remember sitting with him in the empty stadium last week. I know him as a seventeen-year-old, just like me—even though he died when he was fourteen. It is quite strange, I must admit.

Have I been talking to Andy's ghost?

I don't believe in ghosts.

More likely there is a parallel universe where Andy didn't die, and the two worlds are rubbing up against each other. I think I read a sci-fi book about something like that. I wonder if, in the living Andy's universe, I'm the one who died in the fire. Maybe in that universe I was a tiny bit braver, and I ran into the burning house on my own. And maybe the other Andy was not brave enough to come in after me. Does that mean that the Andy I've been talking to for the past few years is a lesser Andy? Possibly. Maybe that is why he didn't come forward and confess to making the phone call. Maybe that is why he let me be kicked out of school. I wonder what he is doing now.

I tighten the miniature clamp that holds the bridge sections together while the glue dries, then start restringing the suspender cables.

Another possibility—I don't know how I could have forgotten about this—is that Andy didn't die in the fire at all. He might have slipped out the back of the house and then, as a joke, hidden out for a few days to watch his own funeral.

It must have been quite a scene when he showed up alive at his parents' door. Why don't I remember that? In fact, I wonder why I haven't seen Mr. and Mrs. Morrow lately. Is it true that they sold the house to George Fuller and moved out years ago? I wonder how George Fuller likes living with a ghost.

I have to trim one of the bridge sections, but I can't find my X-Acto knife. I start looking through boxes. Where did I put that thing? I think the dregs of the Proloftin must still be messing with my memory. Then I open one of the boxes and there it is. Not the X-Acto knife. Something much, much better.

I find the Victorinox Explorer that Andy gave to me. Bright red plastic handle. Seventeen shiny tools. Perfect.

"Douglas?"

"Yeah?"

"What are you doing down there at this time of morning?"

"Working on my bridge."

"How long have you been up?"

"Not long."

"Doug?"

"What?"

"Are you ready to go?"

"I'm busy."

"Whatever you are doing, it can wait."

"No it can't."

"Doug. . ." I hear my father's feet on the basement steps. He reaches the middle of the steps and stops. "Come along, Doug."

"I told you, I'm busy." The bridge is almost complete.

My father descends to the bottom of the steps and stops with the bare bulb burning a few inches above his gray head. He is wearing his long dark gray wool coat and his dark gray wool hat with the brim all the way around. Nobody wears hats like that anymore. Except my father.

"You're just sitting there," he says.

"I'm watching the paint dry. As soon as it's dry I can lay the track."

"Doug, did you take your pill this morning?"

"Mom watched me take it." I had to hold it under my tongue for almost five minutes before I was able to spit the pasty fragments into my palm.

He nods. "Well then, let's get going. We have an eleven o'clock appointment, and it will take us forty minutes to get there."

"Why don't you and Mom go without me?"

"Doug, we're doing this for you. Please come along." He waits, staring at me with a bland expression. Something is very wrong here. Why isn't he yelling?

"I don't want to go."

"I'm sorry, Doug, but that is not acceptable." My father should be shouting, but instead he is talking to me in this quiet, insistent voice.

I don't think I am going to talk him out of this.

34

STATE OF THE ART

We turn into a short driveway leading to a huge iron gate set into a stone wall twelve feet high. A brass plaque attached to the gate reads:

ST. STEPHEN'S ACADEMY
TOMORROW'S ADULTS TODAY

My father gets out of the car and opens a metal box beside the gate. Inside the box is a phone. He speaks into the phone, and a few seconds later the gate swings inward.

We drive through the gate, following a straight, narrow

asphalt driveway through a huge parklike area of rolling grassy hills, thick-trunked oaks, and tall elms. It reminds me of the greenway at Woodland Trails, only spread over a much larger area. After about a quarter of a mile we come to a group of low brick buildings with small windows and few doors.

I do not like this place.

We park in front of the largest and oldest of the buildings.

"I don't like it here," I say. "I want to go home."

My father opens the back door. "Doug, we've driven all the way down here. Let's go inside and take a look, shall we?"

"Why? There's no way I'm going to school here."

Now they are both standing outside the car looking in at me.

"It won't hurt you to look," says my mother.

The man in charge, Dr. Monahan, is average height, average weight, about forty or fifty years old, with a face so ordinary you would never notice him in a crowd. He has brown hair, a brown suit, and brown shoes. His tie is brown also, but his eyes are green and his smile is brilliantly, unnaturally white. I think he looks exactly the way an extraterrestrial would look if he wanted to pass as human. My parents seem quite impressed, but he gives me the creeps. After introducing himself to them, he turns his lighthouse smile on me.

"And this must be Doug. Welcome to St. Stephen's," he says in his newscaster's voice.

"We're just visiting," I say.

"I understand," he says, showing me his teeth. He has a lot of them. "Well, as long as you're here, shall we take a tour of our facilities?"

St. Stephen's Academy is a state-of-the-art facility. I know this because Dr. Monahan tells us so. He tells us so about ten times. He has two favorite expressions: "state-of-the-art" and "I understand." They should call the place the St. Stephen's State-of-the-Art Academy: We Understand.

"Our computer laboratory is state-of-the-art," he says as we enter yet another classroom, this one with several long tables with computers bolted to them every three feet. Like all of the other classrooms we've visited, there are no people.

"And, of course, we have a permanent doctor and pharmacist on staff. Many of our kids have psychological problems, as you know, and we like to make sure that they get their meds."

"Where are all the kids?" I ask. "All we've seen is a bunch of rooms."

Dr. Monahan stretches his mouth into his biggest smile yet. "Of course you'd like to see our other residents, Doug. I understand." He gets another centimeter out of his smile. "All of our students are confined to their rooms at this time. We had a little incident here this morning, and we're giving the kids a few hours to think about it."

"What happened?" my mother asks.

"Two of our students got into a little scuffle after breakfast. A small matter, really, but we have a zero tolerance policy when it comes to unacceptable behavior. Any form of violence results in a lockdown for the entire school. The students quickly learn that individual behavior has repercussions throughout the student body. A valuable lesson."

I say, "A couple of kids get in a fight, so you punish everybody?"

"We give everyone some downtime," he says through his smile. "Would you like to see our auditorium? It has a state-of-the-art sound system. . . ."

The last part of the tour is a walk through the housing facility, a long, low building containing 204 dorm rooms, Dr. Monahan tells us. One room for every two residents. At the building entrance we are greeted by two large men.

"This is Mr. Kloss, our physical education teacher, and Mr. Barrington, who teaches mathematics."

"I thought maybe you were the guards," I say.

They all laugh. Dr. Monahan walks us down the halls. The doors to all the rooms are wide open. I look in as we pass. There are two beds in each small room, with one person sitting or lying down on each bed. They look like ordinary kids at first, but after passing a few rooms I notice that none of them are smiling. Also, they are all wearing the same thing: khaki pants and light blue shirts. And they are all boys.

"Is this an all boy school?" I ask.

"Yes it is," says Dr. Monahan.

"And you have to wear uniforms?"

"That's right. It's much simpler that way, don't you think?"

In fact, I do. I like the idea of not having to figure out what to wear every morning. Everybody has to look equally dorky. But that's the only thing I like so far. I let my parents and Dr. Monahan get a little ahead of me, then stop and stick my head into one of the rooms.

"Hey," I say.

There is only one kid in this room, a bulky Asian kid with a broad face and heavy eyebrows. He looks up at me but says nothing. His eyes are animal empty.

"My name's Doug."

He blinks slowly.

"I'm here visiting."

His eyes lose focus.

"So . . . how do you like it here?" I ask.

He stares blankly into the distance. I think he must be drugged. Probably Proloftin. Or rhino tranquilizer.

"Doug?" Dr. Monahan's hand comes down on my shoulder. "Let's keep on moving. The students aren't supposed to talk to anyone during lockdown."

On the drive home my parents discuss my future. They pretend to be talking to me, but they are really talking to each other.

"It seems like quite a nice facility, dear," says my mother. "I liked Dr. Monahan."

"I thought he was spooky," I say.

"We should be able to afford the tuition for the first year," says my father. "After that, well, we'll see how it goes. We'll see how you do."

"I'm not going," I say.

They ignore me.

"Of course, money isn't really the issue; it's whether the change will be good for you."

"They want you to stay at the school full-time for the first three months. After that you could come home most weekends."

"Why don't I just study at home?"

My words roll right off them.

"I thought the cafeteria menu looked delicious. They have lasagna on Thursdays. Isn't that one of your favorites?"

"We'll need to buy you some new clothing."

"Didn't you think the uniforms looked nice, dear? They don't look at all like uniforms."

"The police have agreed not to pursue charges against you if we can place you at St. Stephen's. We're very lucky that they have an opening."

"I'm not going."

My father turns his head and looks straight at me for the first time all day. "I'm sorry, Doug, but we really don't know what else to do with you."

"Why do you have to do anything?"

His voice goes soft. "You can't spend the rest of your life playing with model trains, Doug."

"Why not?"

"Because that's not the way life works, son."

35

QUALITY OF LINE

My parents plan to deliver me to St. Stephen's Academy next Monday, November 17. That gives me less than seventy-one hours to complete my bridge. Strangely, the closer I get to finishing, the more things I find to do.

For example, while laying the track I notice that some of the suspender cables have mysteriously lost tension. Perhaps the humidity in the basement has changed, or the weight of the track has stretched the cables on one side of the bridge. I readjust them, one strand at a time.

Eventually the bridge is ready, and by Sunday morning I am working on the Madham Special itself. Because a bridge can be inaugurated only once, I want everything to be perfect. I scrape the decals from all the cars and engines and replace them with the sigil logo:

This is in honor of Andy, who should really be here for the inaugural crossing of the bridge. Of course, he might not show up. He's supposed to be dead. But maybe he'll show up. Anyway, I know he'd appreciate the gesture.

Once I get all the cars relabeled—it only takes me about three hours—I get out my Dremel tool and make some alterations to the Coalveyor and the four tank cars.

You would think I'd be very excitable at this point, but the fact is, I'm calm as ice.

My mother makes me try on my new khaki pants and blue chambray shirt. I pretend to be very happy with them, because there is no point in upsetting her.

"I finished my bridge," I say. "I'm sending the first train across it tonight."

"Really! That's wonderful, Douglas! Are we invited to the inaugural crossing?"

So cheerful.

"I'd rather be alone," I say. "I might never get to see it again."

"Now, Douglas, that's simply not true! I'm sure you'll be coming home often."

"You say that now, but just wait till you find out how nice it is when I'm gone."

"Now you're being silly," she says with an expression that means either I hurt her feelings or I spoke a truth she didn't want to hear.

That night after dinner I make my final preparations for the inauguration. I fill the tank cars and the Coalveyor car with cargo. I'm using every car I own for this train, including both locomotives. There are seventeen cars in all.

The track itself is 170 segments long. Each segment is five inches long, so the entire track, connected by the new bridge from East Madham to West Madham, is more than seventy feet in length.

I then go to my room to work on the final sigil. It takes me most of the night to finish this one. I am thinking about mailing it to Mrs. Felko. Even though I'm permanently kicked out of school, I think she would appreciate it. This one has that quality of line she was always looking for.

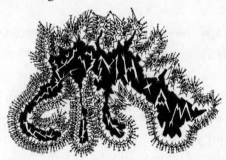

36

DERAILED

At 12:01 A.M. on November 17, the Madham Special, powered by two diesel locomotives, departs the terminal in downtown Madham, heading east through town. It moves down the track past Madham Stadium, where 102 spectators watch the passing of the inaugural train.

This is my gift to the people of Madham—a train day they will never forget. I am bringing them all the drama and excitement of a big Hollywood movie. This is the day of the bridge, the first crossing of the Madham Special.

The train picks up speed as it crosses Oak Street, Elm Street, Poplar Street, Maple Street. At each intersection it is cheered on by crowds of plastic people. Little do they know that the train carries hazardous cargo. The tank cars are filled with red phosphorous. The Coalveyor is piled high with the pink powder. Even the caboose is loaded.

I know I'll never touch these controls again. Once they send me away, I'll be locked up forever. My father will turn my bedroom into a study. George Fuller will sleep soundly through the night. Melissa Haverman will leave her bedroom shades open. Freddie Perdue will have to find some other kid to beat on. Everybody will be happy.

The train enters East Madham. The track curves to the left, climbs a hill, passes Madham Hospital, crosses over itself on a short trestle bridge, and heads back into downtown. Once again the people cheer as it passes the stadium on the other side.

Me? I'll be in my khakis and chambray, veins sluggish with rhino tranquilizer.

The train, picking up speed now, approaches the West Madham Tunnel. There is a danger sign as it enters the tunnel—some problem with the track ahead. The engineer ignores the warning. As the train exits the tunnel it hits a bad section of track. Cars rattle and sway, wheels chatter, phosphorous spills from the Coalveyor onto the steel rails.

Here it comes.

A huge crowd—153 plastic people—is waiting at the entrance to the Andrew Morrow Bridge. The train slows as it begins its crossing. The scene is one of great excitement, anticipation, and joy. Several people have climbed up to the bridge cables to watch the inauguration— troubled teens, no doubt. The mayors of East Madham and West Madham are waiting at the exact center of the bridge, each of them holding a champagne bottle to break across the bow of the locomotive as it passes.

Suspender cables quiver as the train rolls majestically onto the bridge. One of the teenagers falls from the main cable and lands headfirst on the second locomotive. Oh no! He's hurt! The train does not stop. Another boy falls from the bridge, this time into the nameless abyss. Death has come to Madham.

The entire train is now on the bridge. As it nears the midpoint, a crosswind hits the Coalveyor, dusting the mayors and the bridge deck with red powder. The Madham Special continues across the span, leaving the mayors coughing and hacking. It reaches the end of the bridge, where yet another crowd waits, cheering.

The first crossing is successful. The bridge architect sighs with relief as plastic mothers mourn their dead sons. The crowd cheers; the engineer increases speed. The train accelerates through the woods outside of East Madham, past the school, the soccer field, the terminal, the stadium. It barrels through downtown Madham and approaches the West Madham Tunnel at three-quarter speed. Rough track ahead. The engineer boldly increases speed; wheels clatter and spark. There is a bright flash as some of the spilled red phosphorous ignites. The train races on, leaving behind it flaming track. It takes the big curve through the West Madham residential district and again enters the Andrew Morrow Bridge, crossing at near maximum speed. More troubled teenagers fall from the cables, onto the tracks, into the abyss. Phosphorous spills from the

Coalveyor, the train flies across the bridge and into East Madham. The fire spreads from the tunnel into central Madham. The movie theater is in flames, people are melting, an acrid cloud of black smoke mushrooms on the ceiling.

The engineer goes to full throttle.

The Madham Special plows into the flames. For one frozen moment, as the first locomotive emerges from the pillar of flame and smoke, it looks like it will make it through, but a lick of flame catches the coalveyor cargo and the mound of red phosphorous goes off with a tremendous *whoof.* The engineer staggers back. The train continues through the tunnel and toward the bridge, the Coalveyor trailing long, hungry licks of flame.

Will the Madham Special make it across the Andrew Morrow Bridge a third time? It looks good . . . but one of the mayors has fallen onto the tracks. The locomotive plows into him, the train jumps the track, and the red phosphorous on the bridge deck ignites. The suspender cables begin to burn, snapping one after another. Fire races down the bridge, engulfing the passenger cars, the box cars, the tank cars filled with phosphorous.

I look up at the sky and see flames spreading across the basement ceiling.

The bridge is sagging. The fire has spread to East Madham. The air is filled with smoke and shrieks and yelling.

Is that my father's voice?

The first tank car explodes with an ear-cracking, face-stinging bang, louder and sharper than any cherry bomb. The front of my shirt is peppered with bits of burning plastic. A second tank car goes off; I am blinded by the flash.

Is that my ears ringing, or am I screaming?

I am burning and I am blind and I can't find the stairs and I do not know how to get out of Madham.

37

MADHAM

I am sitting in the park, watching the smoke, when a shadow falls across my lap. I look up. It's Andy again.

"Hey, Dougie," he says with a grin.

"Hi," I say.

He sits down on the grass beside my wheelchair. "How's it going?"

"Okay."

"How you feeling?"

"Okay."

We sit for a while. That's pretty much all I do these days. Sit and watch the smoke.

"So . . . what's new?"

"Not much."

"That's cool."

We sit for a while longer, and nobody bothers us. I can hear the train in the distance. You can almost always hear the train, but you never actually see it.

Andy says, "It's nice here."

"I suppose." We sit for a while longer watching the plume of black smoke over the horizon. The fire is always there, always burning, but it never gets closer. Some days I can smell it. They say it's been burning for years.

"Well, I gotta go," Andy says.

"Okay."

"I'll see you later."

"I know."

I watch him walk away. After a while the orderlies come and wheel me back inside through glass doors that read:

MADHAM HOSPITAL

•

BURN UNIT

They wheel me down the long white hall. I look into the rooms as we pass, at all the blackened, melted people. The smell of red phosphorous and burnt plastic is everywhere. My grandfather is here someplace, they tell me, but no one seems to be able to find him. I hope he doesn't find out what I did to his train.

The orderlies lift me from my chair and lay me out on my bed. I stare at the ceiling for a few minutes, then turn my head and find Andy sitting there.

"Hey, Dougie," he says with a grin.

"Hi," I say.

"How's it going?"

"Okay."

"How are you feeling?"

"Okay."

"Nice room."

"It stinks in here."

"You'll get used to it."

"I suppose," I say, but I think that I will never get used to the smell of burnt plastic.

"Well, I gotta go," Andy says.

"Andy?"

"What?"

"Are you really here?"

"Sure I am."

"You were really there all the time, weren't you?"

"You're my best friend. I'll never leave you."

"Okay."

"I'll see you later."

"I know."

HENRY COUNTY LIBRARY SYSTEM
COCHRAN PUBLIC LIBRARY
4602 N. HENRY BLVD.
STOCKBRIDGE. GA 30281